APR 0 5 2004

ß

HOLSTER LAW

ELK GROVE VILLAGE PUBLIC LIBRARY
1001 WELLINGTON AVE.
ELK GROVE VILLAGE, IL 60007
(847) 439-0447

HOLSTER LAW

Bradford Scott

CHIVERS

THORNDIKE

This Large Print edition is published by BBC Audiobooks Ltd, Bath, England and by Thorndike Press®, Waterville, Maine, USA.

Published in 2004 in the U.K. by arrangement with Golden West Literary Agency.

Published in 2004 in the U.S. by arrangement with Golden West Literary Agency.

U.K. Hardcover   ISBN 0–7540–7716 –0 (Chivers Large Print)
U.K. Softcover   ISBN 0–7540–7717–9 (Camden Large Print)
U.S. Softcover   ISBN 0–7862–5947–7 (Nightingale)

The text of this Large Print edition is unabridged.
Other aspects of the book may vary from the original edition.

Set in 16 pt. New Times Roman.

Printed in Great Britain on acid-free paper.

British Library Cataloguing in Publication Data available

ISBN 0–7862–5947–7 (lg. print : sc : alk. paper)

CHAPTER ONE

South of the Red River, which is the border line between Texas and Oklahoma, run two trails. One, called the Lower Trail, is broad and well travelled and follows the course of the river for many miles. The other, known as the Upper Trail, is less travelled. Crossing the Louisiana state line well to the south of the Red, it edges north until for some distance it runs parallel to and within five hundred yards of the Lower Trail but at an elevation of perhaps two hundred feet higher up, following a bench of the hills to the south. A few miles to the west it turns sharply south.

On the Upper Trail where it paralleled the Lower, rode Ranger Walt Slade, he whom the Mexicans of the Rio Grande river villages named *El Halcon*—The Hawk.

Louning easily in the saddle, Slade talked to Shadow, his great black horse.

'Feller, we'll never make it back to the Post today,' he told the black. 'Reckon we'll have to camp out again somewhere, and my provisions are getting mighty low. You're all set, because there's always plenty of grass around, but I can't live on grass like Nebuchadnezzar. That requires a special dispensation of Providence and peculiar digestive organs.'

Shadow, apparently unfamiliar with the

1

unusual gustatory feats of the great Babylonian king of Biblical times, looked dubious. Slade chuckled and rode on, scanning the visible expanse of the Lower Trail.

Not far to the west the broad gray ribbon swerved around a bristle of tall growth to disappear from his view. To the east, a thousand yards or so distant, it flowed from a belt of grove.

Suddenly from the grove burst two horsemen riding at top speed, hunching low in their saddles. Slade watched their approach with interest.

'Those jiggers sure are sifting sand,' he observed to Shadow. 'Looks like they've got places to go and are late getting there.'

On came the hard riding pair; they were almost opposite where Slade sat his horse when another bunch bulged from the grove, seven altogether. They too were skalley-hooting for fair. From their ranks came a guff of smoke; the crack of a rifle reached Slade's ears. He pulled Shadow to a halt, his interest intensified. What the devil was going on, he wondered. Another puff of smoke and another report.

'Wasting lead,' he muttered. 'Mighty small chance of scoring a hit at better than seven hundred yards. What is this all about?'

The fleeing pair flashed past, reached the bend in the trail, swerved around it at top sped and vanished. On came the pursuers. Slade saw a face turned in his direction, caught the glint of a raised rifle. He went sideways in the saddle; but even so, the whining slug fanned his face. With an angry exclamation he hurled himself to ground, sliding his heavy Winchester from the saddleboot as he did so. His eyes, coldly gray, glanced along the sights.

The big rifle bucked against his shoulder; the report sent echoes flying from the hillside.

To Slade's ears came a thin yell as a man reeled, clutching at his saddle horn for support. He dropped the reins, his horse stumbled and went down. Another fell over it, and instantly all was confusion.

Slade withheld his fire. The trigger-happy gent might have made a mistake. And it could be a sheriff's posse chasing a couple of miscreants. Besides, to really throw down on the mess would be too much like shooting setting quail. He contented himself with sending a couple of slugs whining over the tangle as a warning of what would follow if any more shenanigans were attempted.

The two horses scrambled to their feet, apparently none the worse for their tumble. Their riders managed to fork them. The bunch rode on, Slade watching narrowly for a turned head or a lifted rifle. However, they faced to the front and a moment later caromed around the bend and out of sight.

Slade mounted Shadow, slid the Winchester back into the boot under his left thigh and

3

continued his interrupted journey.

'Nice little reception committee,' he remarked to Shadow, 'but I've a notion somebody just went a bit loco. Maybe he thought we were in cahoots with those two hurrying gents in front. Oh, well, let them settle it among themselves, That mixup must have given the pair in front plenty of start to get in the clear so I guess nothing serious will come from whatever the devil it is. June along, horse, we've got a long ways to go and I'll bet it storms before dark. This snake track slides into the hills a little farther on and maybe we can find a hole-up somewhere and spend the night dry.'

The trail, that a little later did enter the hills, was lonely and deserted, but many miles to the east was life, and activity a-plenty.

The Red River was on a rampage. From bank to bank the broad stream was brimful of muddy, swirling water. Huge trees, slowly turning in the current, thrashed the water to a yellow foam with the repeated blows of great branches, the stroke of any one of which would have killed a dozen men. The swollen carcasses of dead animals dotted the flood, grisly reminders of the fate awaiting anything that dared the 'Old Debbil River' in the hour of its wrath. Occasionally some near exhausted criter clinging stubbornly to life could be seen still fighting with ebbing strength to escape the doom that had overtaken its fellows. Watchers on the bank tightened their lips as the body of a saddled and bridled horse swept past. They strained their eyes for a possible but highly improbable glimpse of the rider.

'He was dead forty miles up,' was the unargued verdict.

'Wonder who he was? Did you catch the brand? Looked a mite like the Cross in a Box to me.'

There was no answer from the grimly roaring Red. And the hiss and gurgle of the waters chafing the high banks seemed to hold a chuckle of fiendish merriment.

Overhead the sky was ominous, the blue deadened by a tremulous mist that, as the red ball of the westering sun touched its lower edge against the jagged crests of a range of low hills, discovered lurid saffron edges. And gathering around that bloody sun were dark cumulus clouds banked and tiered, heavy with evil, rising slowly up the long slant of the heavens.

The heat was oppressive, a clammy blanket pressing down on the shrinking earth. The air was heavy, and every now and then there was a strange, elusive shuddering, as if all nature were a living thing suffering recurrent shiverings of dread.

The red rays of the sun smoldered on a countless sea of shaggy backs, glinted from the tossing tips of a myriad needle-pointed horns. The air was filled with querulous mutterings

5

and bleating bawls, and the low, churning sound of a hundred thousand hoofs beating the ground inshort, restless steps that got nowhere, but never ceased.

Thirteen big herds were stranded on the south bank of the crossing. Thirty thousand uneasy mossy horns milled and grumbled. Three hundred equally uneasy cowhands chafed at the delay and cast apprehensive glances at the lowering sky.

Some cheerful prophet of doom remarked on the fact that there were thirteen outfits represented, unlucky thirteen.

'All of the thirteen bunches won't be here come morning,' he predicted dolorously.

The superstitious riders swore at him, and squirmed uncomfortably in their saddles.

'And did you hear that?' he asked by way of making them feel better. 'Was a long ways off, but I heard it. That was thunder on the left. And that is bad. Somebody going to die tonight, mark my words.'

More profanity followed, and covert glances to the left.

To increase the unease, three or four herds of half-wild horses, each numbering between five hundred and a thousand head, added their nervous presence.

A slow cloud of dust rose from where the churning hoofs had pulverized the grass and cut into the dry earth beneath. In the baleful glare from the west, it hung as a rubrous foam over the humped backs of the cows. Each individual particle scintillated like a glowing spark, winking and glittering as it settled slowly only to rise again and eddy in the breath of nearly two score thousand throats.

The individual bunches were held at distances from each other so as to minimize the danger of a mix-up if they took a notion to run. The riders kept them in close herd, frustrating all attempts at straying.

The sun went down in blood. Swiftly the shadows deepened. High in the darkening sky the wind wailed and whimpered. The night closed on the prairie black and sultry and oppressive.

Higher and higher climbed the towering masses of vapor, rolling onward as an army in irresistible might. From the serried ranks thrust thin streamers and huge blotches, like stabbing lances or companies of charging horses. Fantastic and unreal they looked in the flickering glare of the lightning whose flashings were almost incessant.

The grumblings of the uneasy cattle took on a plaintive note, a note of uncontrollable fear. The cowboys swore, and redoubled their vigilance.

Hour after nerve-fraying hour passed, and still the cloud masses climbed and rolled. A low mutter now accompanied the lightning flickers, a mutter that grew to a deep rumble; the swirling heart of the storm was drawing

7

nearer.

The river was rising steadily, as was apparent from the deepening of its growl and the loudening gnaw against its banks. And ever the night grew darker, the heat more oppressive. The thunder grumble was now an incessant rumble, the flares of the heat lightning accompanied by forked tongues that webbed the black heavens with a tangle of glittering snakes. Rain began to fall, steady and fairly heavy.

Suddenly from the churning jaws of the unholy night belched a blinding blaze that poured earthward in a torrent of fire. The prairie was aflame with a frightful radiance, the river a mighty band of molten metal. Then came a crash of thunder like to the falling apart of worlds. Air and earth rocked and shivered.

The cattle burst into terrified bawlings as a second earth-shaking roar split the darkness. But before they could stampede in mad flight, the heavens seemed to fall apart and dissolve in one stupendous sheet of falling water. And with that torrential downpour came a bellowing wind which drove the rain in icy, stinging spears that stabbed and blinded into utter confusion.

Battered by that awful wind, lashed and scourged by the level lances of water, the cattle milled and circled, stumbling blindly this way and that, too numbed to other than bunch and drift. There was no place to run, no place to seek refuge. Turn which way they would, still they faced that terrible rack of the warring elements.

The cowboys were swallowed by the universal confusion. Clinging to their shivering horses, they could but hope that the animals' instinct would preserve them. To attempt to restore something of order to the insane turmoil was ridiculous.

'Some of 'em got away when the big rain started,' a miserable waddie howled to an equally miserable companion. 'I heard hoofs drumming off right after that second big crack. And I got a glimpse of 'em hightailing when the lightning flashed quite a bunch of 'em. I thought I saw some of the boys trying to turn them, but I wasn't sure. Lord! I wish I'd died a-bornin'!'

CHAPTER TWO

West of the Red River crossing, some two miles distant, a range of hills cut the skyline. They were not overly high but were rugged, slashed by canyons and gorges and weed grown dry washes. One canyon, rather narrow, its walls towering cliffs that overhung, bored straight through the range from east to west. Beyond was open prairie for some miles, then

9

more hills and rises and furtive tracks that led to the flat-topped mountains of New Mexico many more miles beyond.

Through this canyon ran the Upper Trail, and on this trail, headed east, rode a thoroughly disgusted Texas Ranger. Slade swore at the wind and the rain, strained his eyes with each lightning flash far something that would provide at least a modicum of shelter, and saw nothing. His tightly buttoned slicker streamed water, and so did Shadow's glossy coat. The north wall of the canyon somewhat broke the force of the wind, but the rain waterfalled into it in a constant deluge. The cliff tops were rimmed with unearthly blue fire as the lightning flashed; the rock walls trembled to the crash of thunder. One moment, the canyon depths were the blackest night, the next they were pools of eerie radiance in which boulder and chimney rock stood out in stark relief.

Slade, although he didn't know it, was no great distance from the east mouth of the canyon when to his ears came a rumbling that was not of the thunder.

'What the blazes, Shadow!' he exclaimed. 'Is there a flood headed this way? If there is and it catches us cramped between these walls, we're liable to mighty soon find ourselves in a place where we'll dry out fast. That is, if cayuses ever get sent Down Below.'

Louder sounded the ominous rumbling.

10

Slade debated what to do, but could arrive at no satisfactory decision. Abruptly he uttered a sharp exclamation; he had catalogued the sound.

'That isn't water, it's cows coming this way, and fast,' he shouted. 'Get going, feller, there's a stampede headed our way!' He whirled Shadow toward the south wall.

The lightning flamed, poured earthward in a cataract of fire that made the canyon bright as day. Slade had a glimpse of shaggy tossing heads and gleaming horns less than three hundred yards to the east. His voice rang out again, rising above the roar of the thunder—

'Trail, Shadow, trail!'

With a plunging bound the great horse shot forward, his irons striking fire from the stones. His long legs flashed like pistons as he slugged his head above the bit and literally poured himself over the ground. Heedless of possible boulders or badger holes in his path, he surged for the canyon wall, the bellowing roar of the charging herd lending wings to feet that very nearly had them anyhow.

Again the lightning blazed. It gleamed on the rolling eyes of the fear maddened cattle. Slade could almost feel their frothing breath. He tore at his slicker to get it open; a blazing gun will sometimes sheer off a charging steer. But before he could reach the big sixes in their carefully worked and oiled cut-out holsters, the herd was upon him. Shadow squealed with rage and pain as a horn rasped his flank. He was all but overthrown by the impact of a hurtling body. Slade jerked his rope free and flailed right and left.

It was the great black's weight and agility that saved them. By a seeming miracle he won through the fringe of the surging mass. In the very shadow of the cliff wall, Slade pulled him to a gasping, snorting halt. The herd roared past them, and he knew the cows would not turn.

And then, when he was congratulating himself on his escape, other things happened.

The lightning flashed, showing the last of the cattle pounding past. It showed also, a band of five or six horsemen riding hard on their tails.

Slade heard a shout. Fire streaked out of the darkness, bullets whined past him, smacking against the cliff, faning his face with their lethal breath. He felt the sting of one that slashed through his coat sleeve and burned the flesh of his arm.

There was no time to get his slicker unbuckled. He grabbed for the stock of his Winchester but the wet stock slipped in his hand. Suction caused the rifle to stick slightly in the water soaked leather saddle boot. Before he could free it, the charging horsemen were past him and swallowed up in the black dark.

Nevertheless, he flung the rifle to his

12

shoulder and sent three wrathful shots screeching toward their unseen backs. He thought he heard a yelp of pain echo the reports but could not be sure. When the lightning flashed again, cows and riders were out of sight around a bulge of cliff.

Slade stuffed fresh cartridges into the magazine of his Winchester and shoved the weapon back in the boot. He glared west through the darkness.

'Shadow, if this don't beat all heck!' he said angrily. 'Here we are attending to our own business and riding back peacefully to the Ranger Post after finishing a hard chore, and twice in the one day we've had lead thrown at us! And for no good reason at all. And, horse, that wasn't any stampede. That was a widelooping or I never saw one. Nobody but cow thieves would shove a bunch along like that through a storm. Looks like Captain Jim knew what he was talking about when he sent word that big drive stranded on the south bank of the Red might bear a mite of watching. Some hellions lifted a bunch under cover of the storm, all right. Well, we've had enough of mavericking around in the dark. We've just got to find a place to hole up till daylight. Ought to be an overhang somewhere or a crack in the rock; let's go see.'

He eased the black horse along the base of the cliff. The overhang shed off much of the rain and against the rock wall the wind was much less severe. A few minutes later a lightning flash revealed a welcome sight.

In the cliff face was a hollow under the jutting overhang that formed a fairly respectable cave and promised to be dry. Along the base of the wall grew a straggle of bushes, the lower branches of which were dead and not yet altogether water-soaked. Another lightning flash showed that in the back of the shadow cave were heaps of twigs and dead leaves carried there by the wind and tinder-dry.

Slade dismounted and groped his way into the hollow, leading Shadow. The cave was but a few inches over six feet in height, barely room for Slade to stand erect and giving Shadow just about sufficient head room if he didn't straighten up too much.

Dropping the split reins, Slade pawed a heap of twigs and leaves to the cave mouth, assisted by accommodating lightning flashes. He broke off an armload of dead branches and pyramided them over the heap. The flicker of a match from his tightly corked flat bottle, the cowboy's waterproof container, and he had a blaze going which he fed with more and heavier branches. This chore attended to, he got the rig off Shadow and tossed it into a corner. He gave the big black a quick rubdown, removed his slicker and deposited it beside the saddle. Batting the water from his broad-brimmed 'J.B.,' he hung it on a convenient knob of rock and rumpled his thick black hair with slim, deeply bronzed fingers.

'Snug as a tick on a sheep's back,' he congratulated Shadow, glancing around with a pleased expression in his long, black-lashed gray eyes. 'Now for some steaming coffee and a snack—you ate earlier so you can hold out till the rain stops.'

He explored his saddle pouches and drew forth the coffee, some bacon and a couple of eggs carefully wrapped against breakage. A hunk of dough-cake left over from breakfast completed the inventory. There was plenty of water available, a lot more than was needed, and soon coffee was bubbling in a little flat pocket and bacon and eggs sizzling in a small skillet.

After eating, Slade rolled and smoked a cigarette. Then he stretched out beside the fire and was almost instantly asleep.

*   *   *

Gradually the wild heart of the storm rolled eastward. The crash of thunder dimmed to a rumble, a mutter. The blaze of lightning became an intermittent flicker. But still the roaring downfall of rain continued undiminished. Not until the first faint gray of dawn brightened the east did it slacken to slowly cease.

In the west a belt of star strewn sky

15

appeared. It widened, dancing points of silver streaming upward after the fleeing clouds. Soon the whole vast arch of the heavens was sown with the corruscating glitter.

But the light in the east was strengthening. Primrose and pink and banded scarlet, it grew and brightened. The stars paled from gold to silver, dwindled to points of fire, and vanished. The rim of the sun appeared. Spears of light flamed to the zenith, darted downward to bathe with brightness a land soaked and sodden with water.

On the drenched river bank was one great herd of more than thirty thousand cattle and several thousand horses, with the demoralized cowboys entangled in the midst of them, too utterly wretched and weary to even swear any more.

The half-broken mustangs romped back and forth through the cattle, neighing for lost friends and adding to the general confusion. The cowhands, gaining a little strength in the sun's warmth, cursed the horses, the cattle, and the day they were born and proceeded to disentangle themselves from the mess. They were drenched to the skin, shivering with cold, utterly worn out. They floundered at the bottom of abysmal disgust and discomfort, with nothing worse to offer.

Or so they thought; but something still worse was awaiting.

CHAPTER THREE

The discovery was made by a puncher who had fought his way from among the humped and steaming cows. Suddenly he jerked his horse to a halt and sat staring with widened eyes, then he let out a yell that turned every face in his direction.

Underneath a bedraggled bush lay two dead men.

'It's John Lake and his range boss, Pete Rasdale!' howled the cowboy as his fellows came pounding up, shouting and cursing.

'Lightning got 'em, eh?' growled a grizzled oldtimer. 'Well, I ain't a mite surprised. I'm still hunting for my hardware. Believe me, gents, I shucked my gun belts off pronto when I heard that first clap; metal attracts lightning.'

Around the dead men, the punchers dismounted. One squatted over the bodies, which lay on their backs, limbs stiff, eyes glazed. Abruptly he leaned forward, peering. He turned his head slowly, presenting a face of stone to the gathering group.

'These fellers weren't hit by lightning,' he said quietly, his voice hard, metallic. 'They've been shot. Look here.'

He pointed to dark stains on the sodden shirts. In the center of each stain was a small round hole.

The cowboy reached out a tentative forefinger, as if to touch an indubitable bullet hole, then jerked it back quickly.

'Gun was held so close to 'em the powder burned their shirts,' he announced. He rose to his feet and faced the steadily augmenting group.

'Where's Lane Branton?' he asked.

There was a sudden hush, followed by low mutterings. Eyes glanced left and right, questions ran from man to man.

'Call him,' said the first speaker; 'maybe he's over the other side of the herd.'

Shouts split the air, repeated several times over. Only the echoes answered.

Again the grim silence, broken only by the stamping of the horses and the grumbling of the cattle warming up in the rays of the sun.

'He wasn't here earlier in the evening, but I reckon he was here when the storm broke,' somebody muttered.

'That's sure for certain,' remarked a lean, bleak-faced old puncher, jerking his head toward the two bodies.

'You ain't got no call to say a thing like that, Perkins,' objected a more fair minded individual.

'I'm saying what I believe,' Perkins replied. 'John Lake was my boss, and I'm saying out plain I believe Lane Branton did for him, and did for poor Pete, too.'

The silence following Perkins' declaration

18

was of a decidedly uncomfortable nature. Men glanced askance at their neighbors. Not a man there who did not know there was big trouble in the making. Very quickly there would be a taking of sides; nearly every man present was a Texan, and a Texan isn't given to doing his arg'fyin' with words. A first class range war could easily cut loose.

A sudden shout on the outskirts of the crowd broke the silence.

'Look there!' an excited cowboy called. 'Look there, riding down the river.'

All eyes were turned upstream. Less than a quarter of a mile distant, two men were riding across the prairie at a fast pace.

'It's Branton and Cliff Hardy, his range boss,' sounded the low mutter.

The two riders veered toward the tense group. They pulled up a few yards distant and dismounted.

One was a young man of about medium height, slender and well formed, with rather good features on the rugged side, but with a truculent look in his eyes and other characteristics that bespoke a quick and possibly uncontrollable temper. His companion was older, with a square jaw, a great beak of a nose and pale, exceedingly bright and alert eyes. His long arms hung loosely by his sides and from them dangled hands that looked like spear points at rest.

The young man strode forward; the bodies

19

under the bush were not visible to him because of the crowd that blocked his view.

'Well, see you had one devil of a time here,' he said.

Silence greeted the remark, silence and the full force of nearly three hundred pairs of eyes focused on his face. He stared with an expression of astonishment.

'Say, what's the matter with you jiggers?' he asked. 'You look as if you'd just come from a burying.'

The lean Perkins shouldered his way to the front. 'Not yet, Branton,' he said. 'So you finally evened the score, you snake blooded sidewinder!'

Branton's eyes widened and on his face was a look of utter amazement.

'Say, have you gone plumb loco?' he demanded. 'What in blazes are you talking about, Perkins?'

'You know blasted well what I'm talking about!' Perkins exploded in a blaze of fury. 'Look there!'

The crowd had instinctively opened up until Branton and his range bass could see the stark forms under the bush. Branton took a step forward, peering.

'Lake!' he muttered stiffly. 'John Lake!'

'Yes, John Lake,' mimicked Perkins. 'You did a finish job, Branton.'

The young man whirled to face his accuser. 'You mean to say you're telling me I did for

20

Lake?' he demanded.

'I ain't telling you anything else,' came the grim reply.

Branton stared. Then his face flushed scarlet. His hand flashed to his holster. Perkins also gripped his gun.

But before either could draw, a man was between them, a tall, broad-shouldered man with hard eyes and a well formed but tight mouth. There was a touch of gray at his temples, a mere silver edging to his otherwise night black hair. His face was sternly handsome and but slightly lined. His voice, when he spoke, was crisp, eventoned and with the assurance of recognized authority.

'Branton,' he said, 'there's no sense in you going off halfcocked. Perkins, you have no call to say what you can't back up.'

'I can back up anything I say,' growled Perkins, tapping his holster.

'Any fool can pull a gun and advertise his lack of brains,' the other countered contemptuously. 'I repeat, you're saying what you can't back up. How do you know Branton killed John Lake?'

'Who else?' retorted Perkins.

'Just the answer I'd expect from you,' said the tall man. 'Who killed Lake is a question. So far I don't see any answer. Just because there was bad blood between him and Branton is no proof that Branton killed him, and you know it. Lake had trouble with other people besides the Brantons.'

Perkins was hot-tempered, but he was also a fair-minded man.

'I'll admit you've got something there, Goodwin,' he replied, 'but I got a right to my own opinion.'

'You have,' assented Goodwin, 'but you have no right to go spouting it around when it deals with as serious a matter as this.'

He turned to Branton, whose face was now paper-white with anger.

'By the way, Lane,' he asked, 'where did you and Hardy just come from?'

'I told you yesterday we were going to ride to the upper crossing for a look,' Branton answered.

'That's right, you did,' Goodwin nodded, 'but how come you took so long to get back? Less than ten miles to the crossing.'

'I know,' said Branton, 'but up there the darndest thing happened to us; I'm still trying to figure it out. We were heading back this way when Hardy spotted a bunch sitting their horses at the edge of a grove like they were waiting for somebody. They were back in the shadow and I reckon anybody who didn't have Cliff's hawk eyes wouldn't have seen them. But he saw them and didn't like their looks.'

'Hardy never likes anybody's looks,' Perkins interpolated caustically. Hardy turned his pale eyes toward him in a speculative way, but the tall Goodwin cut in before the other could speak.

'Shut up, Perkins,' he said. 'Go on, Lano, what are you trying to tell us?'

'Just this,' continued Branton. 'As I said, Cliff didn't like their looks; he 'lowed they were waiting for somebody, all right, and it could be us—funny things happen in this section. I figured he was just seeing things that weren't, but he insisted we turn around and ride back west a ways and see what would happen. We did that, and things did happen.'

'Yes?' prompted Goodwin.

'They sure did,' Branton repeated. 'We'd hardly got going when that bunch came skalleyhooting out of the grove and started throwing lead in our direction; here's a hole in my hat and another one in my sleeve to show for it.'

'And then?'

'And then, seeing as there were seven of them and only two of us, we hightailed,' Branton said. 'Our horses are fast and we drew away from them for a while. But theirs had better staying qualities and they chased us west for miles and miles and began cutting down our lead. Began to look bad for us when something, I don't know what, happened. We bulged around a bend in the trail and a couple of minutes later a heck of a lot of shooting cut loose back around that bend. We didn't wait to find outwhat it meant but kept on going as fast as our bronks would take us. And when the

23

bunch that was chasing us showed again, they were a mile behind. With that much start we took a chance of cutting into the hills, and lost them. We holed up under a cliff during the worst part of the storm but headed back this way while it was still raining.'

Goodwin glanced questioningly at the silent Hardy, whose face was as woodenly expressionless as an Indian's.

'That's right,' drawled Hardy, his voice flat, toneless.

Perkins gave a snort of derision. 'Of all the sheep-dip yarns!' he exploded. 'And do you figure they'd do anything but stick together?' he demanded of Goodwin. 'There were *two* men done in last night, don't forget that.'

The implication was plain. It was answered by the expressionless Hardy, and again his voice was tonelessly in the middle register.

'Perkins,' he said, 'I reckon you'd better fill your hand.'

Seth Perkins, hard man though he was, whitened perceptibly. To do what the stone-faced range boss suggested was tantamount to committing suicide, and Perkins knew it. 'The fastest gun hand in Texas, and he never misses,' was whispered of Cliff Hardy.

But Pace Goodwin again halted the trouble.

'Listen,' he broke in, 'you fellows have got to stop it. This is a cattle drive. Look at that mess over there! It'll take a week to get it straightened out. And there are outfits here

24

that will go bust if those herds don't get through.'

There were sober nods of agreement to the statement of an obvious fact.

'You fellows elected me trail boss for this drive,' Goodwin continued. 'Okay, I'm giving an order: get on the job, everybody. This matter can be thrashed out after the cows are delivered and we're all back in Texas again. Right now we're getting nowhere.'

Again there were nods of agreement.

But the hard-eyed Seth Perkins still hesitated. He hated to give in, even to the supreme authority of an elected trail boss, whose word on the trail is law and not to be countermanded by even an owner. He glared at Lane Branton and his taciturn trail boss, opened his lips to speak.

At that moment a diversion occurred.

'Golly, what a horse!' abruptly burst from the lips of a young cowhand on the outskirts of the crowd.

CHAPTER FOUR

All eyes were turned in the direction of the puncher's gaze. Riding out of the west was a man forking such a horse as folks dream about but don't often see. The exclamations that followed were a deserved tribute to Walt

Slade's Shadow.

The rider was as noteworthy as the splendid animal he bestrode. Very tall, the breadth of his shoulders and the depth of his chest matched his height. His face was lean, deeply bronzed, with a highbridged nose, a rather wide mouth, grin-quirked at the corners, and a powerful chin and jaw. His eyes attracted instant attention. Long, black-lashed, they were clear gray in color. Cold, reckless eyes that nevertheless had little devils of laughter dancing in their depths. The more observant quickly decided that under certain conditions those devils of laughter would very likely be replaced by devils of a very different sort. Nevertheless, they were the kind of eyes that look out gaily on the world and find it good.

As the lone horseman drew near, he was accorded attention unusual for a casual rider on the High Plains. In fact, the cowmen were very glad of something on which to concentrate other than the grim business under discussion; not one but welcomed the diversion. Even the stubborn Perkins doubtless was not sorry of a chance to back down without losing face. A rukus that would disrupt the drive would be but the beginning of endless trouble for everybody concerned; and the man who started it would speedily become very unpopular, to say the least, if he lived that long.

Near the waiting group, Slade drew rein.

'Howdy?' he greeted.

The assembled cattlemen returned the greeting. Slade's gaze wandered over the great milling herd that appeared to extend up and down the river bank as far as the eye could reach.

'Sort of tangled,' he commented.

'They sure are,' Pace Goodwin agreed soberly.

From where he sat his horse, the tall Ranger could see over the heads of the cowboys. His eyes narrowed slightly as they rested on the two stark forms lying in the shade of the bush.

'Somebody get hurt?' he asked casually.

'Sort of,' admitted Goodwin. 'Reckon nothing else will hurt them any more.'

'A rukus?'

'Rukus, the devil!' burst out Seth Perkins. 'It was a snake-blooded killing, feller, and you can lay to that.'

A lane had instinctively opened between Slade and the two bodies. He touched Shadow's neck and rode slowly forward, pulling up beside the bodies.

'When did it happen?' he asked with what nobody would consider other than a casual interest.

'During that infernal storm, of course,' Perkins growled. 'If it had happened before, somebody would have heard the shots.'

'And nobody heard them?'

'How in blazes could anybody hear anything

27

with the whole darn sky bustin' wide open and falling down!' Perkins snorted. 'No, we didn't hear nothing, but I got a—'

Pace Goodwin's shout drowned the rest of the sentence.

'All right!' bellowed the trail boss. 'Everybody on the job; we've got to get those cows untangled. Grab your chuck on the run as soon as it's ready. Get going!'

Long habit asserted itself; the cowboys began moving off to obey the trail boss' orders.

'Perkins, I reckon you Bradded L fellows have a chore to do first,' Goodwin said quietly. 'Might as well get it over with.'

Walt Slade was staring intently at the two dead men. The concentration furrow was deep between his black brows, a sure sign El Halcon was doing some hard thinking, but he said. nothing. He only moved Shadow to one side as the Bradded L hands began their grisly task.

When the bodies were moved onto blankets prepared to receive them, Slade's glance rested for a moment on the ground beneath the bush where they had lain. As the graves were dug and the blanketed forms lowered into them, he dismounted and removed his hat, standing tall and straight beside his great black horse until the burial was complete. He did not offer assistance, for that was not the province of a stranger.

Finally all was done. Two more low mounds had been raised on the prairie, to remain bare until the new grass was grown; there were already many such on the banks of the Red.

The simple head boards were set in place. Slade replaced his hat. Seth Perkins, his hard face lined and weary, his eyes a trifle brighter than usual—perhaps from something on which the sunlight reflected as from a mirror—straightened his back and wiped his hands on his chaps. He bent a searching gaze on Slade, taking in his towering form, his steady gray eyes, the good-humored mouth that somewhat alleviated the tinge of fierceness evinced by the hawk nose above and the prominent chin and jaw beneath.

'Heading for any place in particular, feller?' he asked in casual tones.

'Just riding,' Slade replied. 'Saw this big herd and figured maybe a man could tie onto a job of rope slinging, seeing as there's something of a chore on hand.'

Seth Perkins was evidently satisfied with what his carping gaze had discerned; Perkins knew a tophand when he saw one.

'Reckon that wouldn't be over hard to do,' he said. 'Our outfit is a mite short-handed right now, and getting those cows unscrambled is going to be a hefty chore. I'm sort of in charge now, till we get back to the Brazos. Those two fellers we just planted were John Lake, the owner, and Pete Rasdale, our range boss. My Old Man's name was Perkins. Maw sort of favored Seth for a front handle. Reckon you'll get to know how to holler to the boys in short order.'

Slade supplied his own name. Several of the hands introduced themselves.

'I'll take you over to our wagon,' Perkins volunteered. 'Guess you could stand a bite to eat before tieing into that mess. I'll fix you up with a string of working horses; got plenty of bronks to spare with poor Pete Rasdale and the Boss not here to need theirs any more.'

He stood staring at the two dreary mounds and the lines in his face seemed to deepen.

'I got a still tougher chore ahead of me,' he remarked. 'Got to send word to the Brazos telling Miss Clara about her Dad being done in.'

Slade nodded sympathetically; he felt that words, at the moment, would be entirely out of order.

Seth Perkins shrugged his shoulders, cuffed his hat over one eye.

'Work to be done,' he said. 'Other things can wait for a spell. Blazes! did you ever see such a mess?'

'By the way,' Slade suddenly asked, 'what became of those two men's horses? Looks like they would have been forking them most of the time last night.'

'Why, I don't know,' Perkins replied. 'Didn't think about them. Reckon they're somewhere in that mess over there.'

'Trained saddle horses would hardly mix in

a milling,' Slade remarked. 'And they wouldn't stray far, either, no matter how bad the weather was.'

'Well, I ain't seen 'em,' Perkins said. 'Reckon they'll show up somewhere.'

'Funny those two fellows weren't wearing their slickers, with the rain coming down the way it was,' Slade added.

Perkins stared at him. 'That's right,' he muttered, 'and the sidewinder who did for them would hardly take 'em off afterward.'

'Their shirts wouldn't have been powder burned if they'd been wearing their slickers when they were shot,' Slade pointed out. Again Perkins was forced to agree.

'It was almighty hot last night before the storm,' he observed. 'But just the same I had my rubber on befor ethe rain started— anybody could see it was going to be a drencher and I thought everybody else did, too. Maybe they left theirs off, though.'

'Maybe,' Slade conceded as they moved away from the graves.

The Bradded L cook was a crusty old timer who could kindle a fire and fry a steak under a waterfall, if such procedure were necessary. Despite the weather, he had managed to throw together an appetizing meal. After a liberal helping of prime chuck and several cups of steaming coffee, Slade felt fit for anything. First, however, he gave Shadow another good rubdown before turning him loose to graze.

'Something almighty funny about those killings,' he confided to the big black. 'Those men weren't killed where they were found. They were placed beneath that bush after they were done in; and either before or right after the rain started. The grass where they lay hadn't been beaten down by the rain before they were placed on it. And it is sure for certain they were shot before the rain started. Otherwise the cloth of their shirts wouldn't have been powder burned like it was. And they didn't get it right about the time of that first big thunderclap, which would have drowned the sound of the shots, as the hands seemed to think. They got it before. Somebody jammed the gun muzzle right against them and pulled trigger. Somebody who either was able to get close to them without them suspecting anything wrong or somebody who slipped up on them mighty cleverly.'

Shadow nodded sage agreement. Slade gazed at him with unseeing eyes. What he wondered was why in blazes didn't whoever shot them leave them where they were dragged. The logical conclusion was that they were killed by the bunch he saw shoving the cows through the canyon the night before. Nothing unusual about men being killed by a widelooping bunch they interrupted or came upon unexpectedly. But why should a gang of rustlers drag their victims under a bush and lay them out in order? That had been done, Slade knew perfectly well. His keen eyes had noticed what the others had missed the marks where their spurs cut the ground were plain to see, at least to El Halcon's eyes.

'Shadow,' he concluded, 'it looks like we might have an interesting time ahead of us and some unfinished business to attend to.'

CHAPTER FIVE

When Slade rejoined Perkins, the old cowboy regarded him with a quizzical expression on his lined face.

'Feller,' he said, 'I got a feeling I'm sort of in your debt.'

'How's that?' Slade asked.

'Well,' replied Perkins, 'you happened along at a mighty good time and gave everybody a chance to look you and your horse over and sort of let other things slide. We were mighty close to big trouble, and it's likely that if the ball opened that snake-eyed Cliff Hardy would have gone for me. He's mean and he's lightning fast, and he had me all marked for Number One when the corpse and cartridge session started.

'Far as that's concerned, the whole drive is in your debt, I'd say. Because if things really did bust loose there'd have been taking of sides and, the chances are, ending up with

33

everybody in the rukus. Branton's bunch was with him, and Tom Ward's T Bar W hellions were ready to back up Branton, I'm pretty sure. You may have noticed Ward—the big young feller standing over to one side and saying nothing but seeing everything. Has sort of reddish hair and eyes the color of a grass blade that's just beginning to turn.'

Slade had noticed the tall, wide-shouldered man with the greenish eyes flecked with brown that often go with red hair.

'Ward ain't a killer like Hardy, but he's wild and sure don't step aside for trouble,' Perkins resumed; 'and the boys who ride for him are the same sort. He and Branton have always been sort of friendly, and they both had trouble with John Lake, which kinda ties them together. But let all that slide for the time being, we got work to do and plenty of it. Come along and I'll line you up with horses; reckon you don't need to be told what to do.'

Seth Perkins hadn't exaggerated when he said there was work a-plenty to do; what Walt Slade found the most of in the days that followed was hard work. Unscrambling thirty thousand wild and stubborn longhorns was a chore that wearied bodies, shortened tempers and tied nervous systems in knots. Seth Perkins was a tophand, but he was not of the material of which good range bosses are made; this Slade quickly discovered. And Perkins just as quickly realized that this tall new hand was not only familiar with every angle of range work but was also the sort that soon gathers unto himself all the authority in sight. With the result that before two days had passed, it was Slade and not Perkins who was running the great Bradded L outfit.

'You did a good chore in hiring that big fellow,' Pace Goodwin, the drive boss, told Perkins. 'Wish I'd grabbed him off instead of you.'

The first night with the Bradded L, Slade learned all about the Lake-Branton feud, which began while Austin Branton, Lane Branton's father, was alive.

'The rukus started over what plenty of cow country rows start over—water,' Perkins explained. 'Our south range butts right against Branton's Triangle B north range. Our south range never was any good because there wasn't a drop of water on it; but the Triangle B north, just the other side of a saddleback ridge, had several big springs that flowed plenty; it was Austin Branton's best pasture. That's the way the situation stood for years.'

Perkins paused to roll a cigarette; Slade looked expectant.

'Well,' Perkins continued, 'that's the way things stood till Miss Clara, John Lake's daughter, came back from college last year. While she was off to school she got sort of friendly with a young engineering feller, nothing serious, just friendly. She invited him

35

to amble down and pay the Bradded L a visit. He did, and I sure wish he'd stayed a long ways off. While riding around with Miss Clara, he got a look at our south range and Branton's Triangle B north holding. He told John Lake that if he'd sink what he called an artesian well on our south range there was a good chance he'd get water. Lake wasn't over much for new fangled notions, but Miss Clara arg'fied him into doing it; she could always twist her dad around her finger.

'So Lake started drilling. After they'd gone down quite a way's and hadn't hit no water, Lake wanted to give it up, but Miss Clara made him keep on sinking that hole.'

'And he finally hit water?'

'I'll say he did!' Perkins declared emphatically. 'All of a sudden a squirt of water shot out of that hole ten feet in the air, just a'bilin', and it kept on shooting. We had water, plenty of water, more than we needed. It formed a regular creek that followed the north side of the hogback and finally tumbled into a canyon miles over to the west.'

Shortly before the loss of his father's ranch, due to recurrent droughts and blizzards and the general doldrums of the cattle business, followed by the elder Slade's untimely death, Walt Slade had graduated from a famous college of engineering. He had planned to take a post graduate course to round out his education, but the untoward circumstances

36

had rendered that impossible for the time being. Captain Jim McNelty, the famous commander of the Border Battalion, had suggested it might be a good idea for Walt to come into the Rangers for a while and study in spare time. Slade thought so, too, and accepted the Captain's offer. Long since he had gotten all he needed and more from private study; but Ranger work had gotten a strong hold on him and he was loath to sever connections with the famous corps of law enforcement officers. He'd stick with the Rangers for a while. He was still young and there was plenty of time to be an engineer. So, with an engineer's knowledge of such matters, he knew pretty well what was coming.

'Well, that was fine for the Bradded L,' Perkins pursued, 'but I'll be dadblamed if every spring on Branton's north range didn't dry up pronto. All of a sudden his north range didn't have a lick of water, and you know what that means in dry cow country. Did you ever hear of anything to beat it?'

'A perfectly natural result,' Slade replied, 'the well drew off the underground flow that supplied Branton's springs. Nothing unusual about it; it has happened before.'

'Well, this time it happened once too often,' Perkins grunted. 'It sure kicked up one unholy row and set Austin Branton to pawing sod for fair; he rode up to our casa mad as a short-tailed steer in fly time. I figured a shooting was

37

going to come off. John Lake was a salty old jigger and Austin Branton could have cut some notches on the handle of his gun, if he'd been the sort that cuts notches. He accused Lake of stealing his water and spoiling his best pasture. He wouldn't listen to reason when Lake and the engineering feller tried to point out how the mess could be cleared up.'

'By channeling through the ridge and sending the overflow onto Branton's land,' Slade interpolated.

'Uh-huh, that would have done the trick, though it would have been a hefty chore,' Perkins acceded. 'But Lake never got a chance to explain to Branton. Old Austin got madder and madder and called Lake plenty of hard names. It was mighty hot weather and he got so mad that all of a sudden he tumbled over with a stroke of some sort. Two days later he was dead.'

Slade whistled through his teeth. Again he knew perfectly well what was coming.

'Young Lane Branton was mighty close to his father and is as quick on the trigger as old Austin ever was,' Perkins resumed. 'He flew into a plumb crazy rage, braced Lake in town and accused him of being responsible for his dad's death. He said some mighty hard things that didn't set over well with John Lake. There really would have been a shooting if Sheriff Cooney hadn't happened to be on hand and busted it up. Branton rode back to his spread

38

calling Lake a snake-blooded killer and he never showed up at the Bradded L casa from that day to this, although he used to be around there plenty; him and Miss Clara being mighty good friends.'

'Lake and Branton never made up, then?'

'Nope,' Perkins replied soberly. 'Between you and me, I've a notion John Lake would have liked to after he cooled down a bit. I think he was just waiting for Lane to make the first move; but Lane never made it. He's stubborn as a blue-nosed mule and Lake never got a chance to even talk with him. Pace Goodwin brought word that Branton was making threats and vowing to get even, but Lake just laughed that off, said Branton was j just letting off steam. At the time, I thought maybe that was so, but now I'd say Goodwin was right and John Lake was wrong.'

'And you figure Branton killed John Lake— murdered him—because of the row?' Slade asked curiously.

'I sure do,' Perkins growled.

Slade let the full force of his level gray gaze rest on the cowboy's face.

'But you have absolutely no proof that Branton killed John Lake,' he warned.

'No, I ain't got no proof,' Perkins admitted, 'but I sure got my notions. Maybe I wouldn't feel so sure about it if Branton hadn't hired that snake-eyed Cliff Hardy and made him his range boss. Hardy is a killer and plumb deadly.

He's got a reputation, although so far he's kept from stretching rope. I 'low Branton figured to make troubles sooner or later and hired Hardy to back up his play. And they were somewhere out of sight last evening before the storm broke, and when they showed up just a little while before you did, they told a cock-and-bull yarn about riding to the upper crossing and being chased way west by a bunch.'

'I believe I can substantiate that part of the story,' Slade said thoughtfully. 'Yesterday when I was riding the Upper Trail quite a ways west of here, I saw two fellows being chased by a bunch of seven. The distance was too great to distinguish features, but one of the pair in front was riding a roan and the other a dun.'

'Branton was riding a dun and Hardy a roan when they showed up this morning,' Perkins muttered. 'But who the devil would be chasing 'em, and why?'

'There are bands along this river that would murder a man for his horse and what he might chance to have in his pockets,' Slade answered obliquely.

'You're right about that,' Perkins conceded. 'By the way, Branton said that after they skalleyhooted around a bend they heard a lot of shooting back behind, and that when the bunch showed again they'd lost a lot of ground, enough to enable him and Hardy to take to the hills and get in the clear.' He looked at Slade suggestively.

40

'Yes, they heard shooting,' the Ranger agreed. 'One of the bunch threw lead at me, for no reason at all, so far as I could see.'

'And you threw some back?'

Slade nodded. 'And if you have any notion that the bunch might have come from here, you can keep your eyes open for a gent who doesn't look too spry,' he added. 'I think I marked one of them a bit; he yelled and grabbed leather. Let the reins drop and his horse fell with him and pitched another one; that's mostly what held them up. He was able to fork his bronk when it got on its feet, though, so the chances are he wasn't hurt badly.'

Perkins swore gloomily. 'Things are getting more mixed up by the minute,' he complained, his brow wrinkling into querulous lines.

Slade believed he had sown a seed of doubt in Perkins' mind and was content to leave it to grow a bit; he deftly changed the subject away from Lane Branton.

'I believe you said something about a man named Ward having had trouble with Lake?' he prompted.

'Uh huh, Tom Ward,' answered Perkins, 'As I said before, I don't consider Ward a killer type like Cliff Hardy, but he's sort of wild. Likes whiskey and cards and has an eye for a pretty girl.'

'None of which are particularly serious vices if not carried to extremes,' Slade smiled.

41

'Reckon that's so,' Perkins agreed. 'The redeye he drinks don't ever seem to affect him much and he plays a good hand of cards and don't waste too much time gambling.'

Slade suppressed a chuckle; he had a feeling that Seth Perkins was a bit of a misogynist and didn't press for an opinion on the girl angle.

'Ward used to visit the Bradded L *casa* quite a bit, like Lane Branton did,' Perkins resumed. 'I figure he sort of liked Miss Clara. John Lake never objected to Lane coming around, that is, before the row, but he always looked sort of sideways at Ward because of his mavericking. And after Ward and his bunch of swallerforkers got into a rukus at Warton, the county seat, and wrecked a saloon and plugged a couple of jiggers and got thrown in jail for a week, he told Ward he didn't want him hanging around the *casa* any more. I was there when it happened, Ward didn't say anything, but I saw those green eyes of his get sort of smoky, and he looked Lake up and down, slow and hard. Nope, didn't say a thing. Just turned around and walked to his horse and rode off without looking back. I figure inside he was peevish as a teased snake. Anyhow, when Sully Davis—he's the big rawboned feller with the scar on his cheek—sort of twitted him about it in town that night, Ward knocked him cold. Sully didn't come to for ten minutes. Yes, him and Lane Branton sort of have something in common, and they always were kinda friendly, so I figure Ward will back Branton if a row breaks.'

'I see,' Slade said thoughtfully. 'Well, the chore of work ahead of them should tend to cool everybody down a bit, and with the drive to Dodge City ahead of them, they'll be sort of busy.'

'You're right about that,' Perkins acknowledged.

However, Slade was not as optimistic about the situation as he led Perkins to believe. At the moment, it was the hot-tempered, impulsive Perkins himself who gave him most concern. Perkins was firmly convinced that Lane Branton was responsible for John Lake's death and it would be difficult to change his mind unless he could be shown positive proof to the contrary.

There was an angle involved that it appeared Perkins was not aware of; the, to Slade's mind, incontrovertible fact that somebody had taken advantage of the confusion attendant to the storm to run off a sizeable herd of cows, several hundred, Slade estimated. Whose cows they were would not be ascertained until the herds were separated and a tally taken. Then, Slade feared, more trouble would cut loose. He was right.

CHAPTER SIX

At about the same time Slade was conversing with Perkins, he himself was under discussion in another quarter.

'I'm scared we're in for trouble, Lane,' Cliff Hardy, the Triangle B range boss, told his employer. 'Mighty funny, that big jigger Slade riding in from nowhere in particular like he did and tieing up with the Bradded L pronto. I have a notion Perkins, or Lake, sent for him to do their gun slinging for them if it comes to a showdown. That feller's bad, or I'm a lot mistaken, and I don't often make mistakes with his kind. A gunfighter, all right, a two-gun, quick-draw man or I never saw one. Don't try to buck him, Lane, you wouldn't have a chance. Leave him to me if something starts; I've a notion I can take care of him.'

'Maybe,' Branton replied. Hardy shot him a quick glance.

'You talk like you ain't exactly sure,' he commented. 'Seen me in action, ain't you?'

'Uh-huh,' Branton said. 'Uh-huh, and I know you're good, mighty good, but I heard something you should know about, so that you'll understand who you're up against. Tom Ward recognized that big hellion, said he saw him once down in the Big Bend country. Got a reputation of being a mighty smart owlhoot

44

nobody has ever been able to pin anything on.'

'Huh!' scoffed Hardy. 'Those brush poppers are always getting a reputation for being tougher and badder thanthey really are.'

'Uh-huh,' Branton conceded soberly, 'that's so, all right, but Ward mentioned that jigger's name, the one the Mexicans along the Rio Grande gave him, and it fits. Cliff, Tom Ward swears that jigger is El Halcon.'

'*El Halcon!*' Hardy ejaculated. 'Sure Ward ain't making a mistake?'

'Well, he didn't talk like he was making one,' Branton replied.

Cliff Hardy's pale eyes grew speculative. 'El Halcon,' he repeated. 'The Hawk! Yep, I've heard of him, heard plenty, and Lane, you know I've always had a sort of hankering to try out with that jigger. Oh, I don't mean I've got anything against him, for I haven't; I never have anything against anybody. I just got a sort of professional interest in him as it were. They say he's greased lightning on the draw and never misses, but I've a notion maybe he's exaggerated.'

'Maybe,' admitted Branton, still dubious, 'but there's something about those eyes of his that makes you feel he's looking right inside of you and if there's anything you want to cover up, he'll see it, and figure you right.'

Hardy shot him another of his quick glances. 'Getting nervous?' he asked softly.

'Not exactly,' Branton replied, 'but I'm

afraid a lot of folks are—thinking. Which, under the circumstances, is enough to make a man feel a bit jumpy.'

Hardy shrugged his shoulders and deftly changed the subject. 'Wonder what Miss Clara will have to say?'

'Hard to tell,' Branton answered wearily. 'Not hard to guess, though, the kind of a yarn Seth Perkins will have sent her.'

'Perkins will go too far someday,' Hardy predicted.

'Want a bit of advice?' Branton asked.

'Can't say as I want any, but I'll listen,' Hardy replied. 'What's on your mind?'

'Just this,' Branton said, 'forget all about Perkins and concentrate on Slade; he's the man we've got to watch. Tom Ward thinks so, too.'

'For once I've a notion you're both right,' Hardy conceded.

*   *   *

Pace Goodwin, excellent trail boss though he was, had been optimistic when he estimated it would take a week to straighten out the mess left by the storm. A full ten days elapsed before the mixed cows were unscrambled and assembled at their respective holding spots.

Meanwhile Slade had ample opportunity to study Lane Branton and his *amigo* Tom Ward. And he arrived at the conclusion, tentatively at

46

least, that Ward was the more dangerous man of the two, if there was any reason for him to be dangerous. Brandon was quick-tempered, explosive and impulsive, swift to speak his mind. Ward, on the other hand, was almost taciturn and quiet. Slade felt that he was the sort that would bottle up resentment inside himself and give no outward expression of his state of mind. And when that kind, Slade had learned through experience, did explode, it was apt to be with devastating violence. Also Ward might be capable of coldly plotting an action and carrying it to a successful conclusion in a quietly efficient manner. And whoever killed John Lake and Pete Rasdale, his range boss, had to all appearances carefully planned the deed in advance.

Not that Slade had formed any definite conclusion concerning Tom Ward or Lane Branton relative to the killings of Lake and Pete Radale, but he was a Ranger and two murders had been committed. As a Ranger it was his duty to apprehend the culprits, and as a Ranger he must not overlook anything that might lead to their apprehension. So far as he had been able to learn, Ward and Branton were the only persons among the near three hundred present who had any reason to hold a grudge against John Lake. How much the intensity of that grudge was colored by Seth Perkins' imagination he could not at the moment know; but he did not lose sight of

47

the fact that so far he had heard only Perkins' version of the story of what could have led up to the killings.

He still did not overlook the possibility that Lake and Rasdale might have been killed by the rustlers who, in his opinion, ran off a herd the night of the storm. But why in blazes would wideloopers interrupted in the course of their nefarious activities take the trouble to move the bodies from where the crime was committed and carefully lay then out where they were found! Slade didn't have the answer to that one.

Finally the cutting out was finished and the tallying began; and when the tally was completed, Seth Perkins' face was black as a thundercloud.

'A good five hundred head short, all prime beef critters!' he stormed. 'Hank Sybold was right when he 'lowed he saw a bunch hightailing it with jiggers shoving 'em along that night right before the storm broke. I begin to see how Lake and Rasdale got done in; the sidewinders were doing a chore of widelooping, too!'

A sudden hush fell as Perkins glared at Lane Branton. The cloud that had lowered over the drive since the night of the storm was ready to burst in flame and blood.

Lane Branton took a step toward Perkins, his face livid with anger. Beside him, arms swinging loosely at his sides, was Cliff Hardy,

48

his wooden-faced range boss.

'We might as well get this over with,' Branton said in a dry, hard voice. 'Perkins, put up or shut up!'

Both men dropped their hands to their belts.

'Hold it!'

Men jumped as Walt Slade's voice rolled in thunder. All eyes turned in his direction. Slade's face was bleak as chiselled granite. His eyes no longer glowed with the gay reckless light the cowboys had become accustomed to associate with them. Now they were icily gray, with little red flickers in their depths—the terrible eyes of El Halcon!

'Hold it!' Slade repeated. 'This blasted foolishness has gone far enough. Perkins, you and Branton both shut up and go about your business.'

There was an instant of silence. It was broken by Cliff Hardy's flat, toneless voice—'

'What the devil business you got horning in on this?'

Slade's reply was brief and to the point. 'I'm making it my business, Hardy—and ready to back it up.'

Men caught their breath and stood stiffly rigid. Cliff Hardy's face remained expressionless. It still remained expressionless as his hand flashed down with blinding speed.

But it was not expressionless a split second later as he reeled backward, staggering and scrambling, clutching at his blood spurting right hand. His gun, the lock smashed, one butt plate knocked off, lay a dozen feet distant.

Slade spoke through the smoke wisping from the muzzle of his Colt.

'Don't try it again, Hardy,' he said quietly. 'Next time you'll get more than a skinned hand. You're too darn fast to take chances with.'

Cliff Hardy glared, his face convulsed with rage and pain. Then abruptly his countenance smoothed out to its normal impassiveness. In his pale eyes a sly and humorous twinkle showed. And for the first time in the memory of anybody present, the tense cowhands saw him grin.

'Feller,' he said, a suspicion of a chuckle in his voice, 'there ain't going to be no next time, not where you're concerned. You don't happen to be Buckskin Frank Leslie growed to about seven feet, be you? He's the only jigger I ever heard tell of I figured could shade me.'

With a nod that was almost friendly, he turned, wrung his skinned and bleeding knuckles, picked up his smashed gun and stalked off.

There was a hissing sound as some three hundred men exhaled the breath they had been unconsciously holding.

About three hundred pairs of eyes were focused on Walt Slade, but he instinctively felt one concentrated gaze. He turned slightly to see Pace Goodwin, the drive boss, regarding him intently, a strange expression on his face. It was gone instantly, however, as the drive boss took belated charge of the situation.

'I hope everybody's satisfied,' Goodwin said. 'If they are, suppose we get back to work. We cross the river in the morning and there's still plenty to do.'

And a moment later, Tom Ward remarked to Lane Branton, 'Reckon you'll remember now what I told you and believe he's El Halcon with the fastest gun hand in Texas. Or, in my opinion, anywhere else.'

'I'm not arguing,' Branton replied, 'and I reckon Cliff isn't either. I've got good eyes and I was looking at him, but I didn't see him pull; that gun just happened in his hand. And the cold nerve of that hellion! Taking that chance and shooing Hardy's gun out of his hand! Suppose he'd have missed?'

'If he'd missed,' Ward replied dryly, 'I've a notion he would have "*missed*" about three inches to the left.'

CHAPTER SEVEN

A poll of all present would doubtless have achieved a verdict that there had been plenty of excitement for one day; but it wasn't over yet.

51

Just as the hands were gathering around the chuck wagons, a lone rider was observed speeding up from the south. As the racing horse drew near, the rider was seen to be a girl, a tall, level-eyed girl with hair the color of ripe corn silk.

'Oh, good gosh!' Seth Perkins suddenly wailed. 'It's Miss Clara!'

He leaped to his feet and waved his hat. The girl rode forward and drew rein. She dismounted with lithe grace as Perkins hurried to meet her.

'Ma'am, why'd you come here?' he sputtered.

'I had to, Seth,' the girl replied quietly. 'When Chuck Lurton rode in with the word of—what had happened, I just had to. I was praying all the time I'd get here before you crossed the Red.'

'Well, you're here,' Perkins said heavily.

'Chuck didn't tell me much,' the girl continued. 'He just said Dad met with a bad accident and didn't pull through. That's all I could get out of him. How did it happen, Seth?'

Perkins twisted his hat miserably. He shot an appealing glance at Slade. But before either could speak, a man strode forward and bowed courteously to the girl; it was Pace Goodwin.

'How are you, Clara?' Goodwin said. 'Mighty glad to see you but sorry it had to be at a time like this.'

52

With a nod to Sade and Perkins, he took the girl by the arm and gently led her aside.

Perkins heaved a sigh of relief. 'That helps,' he muttered to Slade; 'let Pace tell her. Pace has a way with women, and I always figured he was sort of sweet on Miss Clara. John Lake didn't approve of him, though, that is for Miss Clara. He used to say Pace was old enough to be her father. Pace gambles considerable, too, and that didn't set over well with Lake. He liked Pace and respected him as a cowman, but I don't figure he'd have been over pleased if Miss Clara had taken him. I know he told her as much.'

'And what did she say?' Slade asked.

'She just smiled, same as she would when Lane Branton or Tom Ward was mentioned. I figure she sort of liked all of 'em, which one best I couldn't say. I'm pretty sure she felt mighty bad over the row between her dad and the Brantons.'

Slade nodded. His eyes rested speculatively on the pair standing a little ways off, talking earnestly in low tones. He saw the girl shudder, pass one slender sun-golden hand across her eyes.

'Yes, Pace will do a good job of breaking things easy,' Perkins said. 'He's an educated feller and knows how to talk well.'

'Goodwin one of the oldtimers down in your section?' Slade asked idly. Perkins shook his head.

'Nope, he showed up in the section about a year or so back,' he replied. 'Come from Arizona, I believe. Bought the Scab Eight spread from the Widow Harness, who wanted to go to Dallas and live with her daughter. Spread was sort of run down, but Pace soon made it a going concern. Brought in good stock and kept adding to his herd. Good business man. It was Pace organized this big drive. He said there would be a market in Dodge City for one more big shipping. Most folks figured the northern drives were about ended, but Pace persuaded the other owners that one more could be handled. I've a notion he was right.'

'I think he was,' Slade said, 'but I wouldn't be surprised if we're seeing the last really big drive to roll north. The railroads are coming close to the grazing land from every direction and soon it won't pay to make the northern drive, and there'll be no reason to make it, with plenty of shipping facilities nearer home.'

'Reckon that's so,' Perkins agreed. 'Here comes Miss Clara back. She's a real gal and's taking it like a thoroughbred.'

Clara Lake was indeed a true daughter of the range. And the rangeland is all too used to death sudden and sharp. Her fine eyes were weary and pain filled when she returned to the campfire after saying goodnight to Pace Goodwin; but there were no tears. She accepted a plate of food from Perkins and ate with appetite.

After Perkins had introduced them, Slade walked away, on the pretext of looking after his horse.

'Things are getting more mixed up all the time,' he confided to Shadow. 'I'd figured we'd head for home and a rest, but it doesn't seem to be working out that way. I'm very much afraid we've got another long and hard ride ahead of us.'

Slade spoke in a mournful tone, but there was a gleam in his eye that belied it. Shadow snorted derisively and did not appear at all depressed. Slade chucked and tweaked his nose. Shadow answered the indignity with a baring of milk-white teeth. Having mutually affronted each other they stood in friendly silence till Slade heard Perkins calling him to return to the camp.

'I'm going over to the wagon to fix Miss Clara a place to sleep,' Perkins explained. 'Walt, you stay and talk to her.'

After Perkins departed, the girl regarded Slade in silence for a moment, a peculiar expression in her eyes.

'Seth told me you prevented serious trouble here today,' she suddenly observed.

'Oh, I expect it wouldn't have amounted to much,' Slade deprecated.

'From what Seth said, I've a notion it would have,' Clara Lake differed. 'I want to thank you.'

Slade smiled, the flashing white smile of El Halcon that women, and men, found irresistible.

'That's ample recompense for anything I may have been able to do,' he said.

'I would have felt terrible if anything had happened to Seth or Lane Branton,' she replied.

'You think rather well of young Branton, then?'

'Yes, I do,' she answered. 'I like Lane very much and it hurt me when he and Dad had trouble and Lane stopped coming to visit.'

She hesitated. Slade was silent, feeling sure there was more to come.

'Seth appears convinced that Lane was responsible—for my father's death,' she said.

'Perkins has no business saying a thing like that,' Slade instantly countered. 'He bases his assumption on the fact that Lane Branton and your father had a disagreement, with nothing tangible to bolster his accusation.'

The girl regarded him thoughtfully for a moment.

'Do you believe Lane Branton killed my father?' she asked abruptly.

'Miss Lake,' Slade replied, 'I have no reason to believe Lane Branton had anything to do with your father's death.'

She apparently did not perceive that his answer verged on the ambiguous; which was what Slade intended.

'I'm glad to hear you say that,' she said, adding with apparent irrelevance, 'People say Cliff Hardy is a dangerous man.'

'He is,' Slade agreed, adding reflectively, 'but somehow I have a feeling that he is dangerous only when the other man is standing up to him and ready to take his chances. I have nothing concrete on which to base such an estimate; I'm prompted by just something in the nature of intuition, I suppose. And intuition is generally conceived as being a feminine prerogative.'

The inscrutable expression was back in her eyes where she spoke again.

'You are a—cowhand, Mr. Slade?'

'I'm working as a cowhand for you, am I not?' Slade parried.

'Yes, I suppose you are,' she said slowly. 'Or so Seth Perkins gave me to understand. He also said that you have been to all practical purposes running the outfit since he hired you and if it were not for you, the work would not have been accomplished so speedily and efficiently.'

'I'm afraid Seth tends to exaggerate,' Slade smiled.

'I've always found him apt to lean in the other direction,' she differed. 'Seth is more liable to be critical than laudatory. But this time he was lavish in his praise. You appear to have, well, sort of hypnotized Seth. I wonder if you always have that power over people; I

57

admit I am aware of it myself.'

Slade's laughter rang clear and musical, his strangely colored eyes dancing. Under his regard, Clara Lake blushed rosily, and though she was undoubtedly far from a smiling mood, her answering smile was wide enough to show a dimple at each corner of her sweetly shaped mouth.

Seth Perkins strode into the circle of firelight. 'All set for you, Ma'am,' he announced. 'You figure to head back for the Brazos in the morning?'

'No, Seth,' the girl replied. 'I'm going along with the drive.'

'It'll be a tough chore,' Perkins warned. 'We got other rivers to cross 'sides the Red.'

'I've crossed rivers before,' Clara Lake said quietly.

Perkins shrugged. 'You're the boss now,' he conceded. 'When you talk, you hand out the powders.'

Shortly afterward, Pace Goodwin put in an appearance. He squatted beside the fire and engaged the girl in conversation; he spoke exceedingly well, Slade thought, and was undoubtedly a man of more than a little education and culture. Abruptly he turned to Slade and asked the question that Slade instinctively felt was his real reason for returning to the Bradded L camp.

'Reckon you'll be trailing your rope now the chore here is done?'

Slade smiled slightly and shook his black head. 'No,' he replied. 'I think I'll go along with the drive, if Seth figures he can use me.'

Goodwin smiled and nodded, but before he could comment, Seth Perkins burst out—

'Can I use you! But I reckon Miss Clara has the say.'

'I think the drive will have a better chance to get through with Mr. Slade—in charge of the Bradded L herd,' she decided instantly.

Goodwin shot Slade a keen glance and the latter wondered if he interpreted a personal interest on the part of the girl in her newly appointed range boss, and possibly resented it. However, Goodwin merely nodded approvingly.

'I'm mighty glad to know you're going along,' he said. 'Perhaps you can hold down these hotheads who hanker for trouble. I've a notion nobody will care to start any after the exhibition we had today. I'm pretty sure Cliff Hardy won't, and Branton won't without Hardy to back him up.'

Slade glanced at the girl and saw her red lips tighten the merest trifle.

'And Tom Ward won't if Branton doesn't initiate it,' Goodwin added.

Again Slade noted a slight tightening of Clara Lake's lips. He sensed that the trend of the conversation was distasteful to her. But before he could deftly change the subject, Goodwin made another remark.

'So I guess that leaves only you, Perkins, to tighten your cinches,' he said.

Perkins flushed and started to reply, but Clara Lake's cool voice interrupted.

'I'll vouch for Seth not stirring up trouble, Pace,' she said quietly.

'Then it looks like we may have peace from here to Dodge City, that is so far as the drive members are concerned,' Goodwin said. 'Now if we can just beat off the rustlers that are going to be hanging on our flanks watching for a chance to run off a herd or two.'

'You contemplate having trouble with wideloopers?' Slade asked, steering the conversation into more acceptable channels.

'Well, if you've ever made the northern drive before, you shouldn't have to ask that,' Goodwin replied.

'I thought perhaps things had cooled down a bit in recent years,' Slade replied evasively.

'They haven't,' Goodwin said shortly. 'With fewer herds going north, the boys in the hills are getting hungry; we'll be lucky if we get to Dodge without having trouble.'

'I expect we can take care of any that comes our way,' Slade predicted cheerfully.

'I hope so,' Goodwin said. 'Well, good night, everybody, I'm going to try and get a little rest. We want to be rolling early in the morning, against the chance of this infernal river taking a notion to act up again. It can do that mighty fast when it takes a notion.'

'You're darn right,' agreed Perkins. 'Good night, Pace.'

The camp was early to sleep, for everybody was tired out and there was a hard day ahead.

'I sure hope it don't take a notion to rain some more,' was Seth Perkins' last worrying remark as he gazed at the clouded sky, in which no stars were visible.

Clara Lake lingered a moment after Perkins had departed to seek his bed roll.

'I'm very, very glad you consented to go along, Mr. Slade,' she said.

'I had planned to, but not until tonight did I realize how pleasurable a chore it was going to be,' Slade replied.

She colored prettily, then looked him straight in the eyes, and there was understanding in her gaze.

'Yes, pleasurable for you,' she said softly, 'but for the girl—only memories.'

She was gone before a Ranger knocked slightly off balance was able to frame a suitable reply.

CHAPTER EIGHT

Walt Slade waited until he was sure all were asleep except the slowly riding night hawks who guarded the herds. To evade the drowsy watchmen in the black dark was an easy chore.

He got the rig on Shadow, led the big horse until they were out of hearing, then mounted and rode west along the river bank. A mile or two above the upper crossing, on the north bank of the river, he knew there was a railroad station.

Making the crossing without difficulty, he rode on west until he saw the glow of light that marked the station. A telegraph operator drowsed over his clicking instrument; he looked up quickly as Slade entered.

'I would like to send a short message,' Slade announced without preamble.

The operator stared somewhat askance at El Halcon's towering form.

'I don't know cowboy,' he hesitated. 'This is a railroad telegraph and unless it is an emergency—'

Slade made no verbal reply. He slipped something from a cunningly concealed secret pocket in his broad leather belt and laid it on the operator's table.

The operator stared at the glittering object—a gleaming silver star set on a silver circle, the feared, honored and universally respected badge of the Texas Rangers. He raised his eyes to Slade's face.

'Guess it's an emergency,' he chuckled. 'Shoot!'

The message Slade addressed to Captain James McNelty, Ranger Post Headquarters, was briefly laconic. It read—

'It happened in Texas.'

'There should be a reply in a couple of hours if Captain Jim isn't out sashaying around somewhere,' Slade said as the operator opened his key.

The something more than an hour before a reply came passed pleasantly enough. The operator made coffee on a little stove, broke out sandwiches and insisted Slade join him. He was a jovial and talkative soul but wisely refrained from asking any questions.

When the reply came, it was as laconic as the message which prompted it—

'Anything that happens in Texas is your business.'

Slade chuckled as he went to get his horse. He had all he needed, a go-ahead sign from Captain Jim no matter where the trail led.

'Feller, we don't pack any authority north of the Red except holster authority, but I reckon that will be enough,' he told Shadow as he recrossed the river and rode back to camp.

*   *   *

The following morning the drive rolled northward. By the orders of the trail boss, Pace Goodwin, the herds were widely spaced.

'We don't want another mix-up like we had here,' he explained. 'We've still the Canadian, the Cimarron and the Arkansas to cross.'

Slade received the orders without comment, but Seth Perkins shook his head dubiously.

'I reckon Pace is right,' he confided to Slade, 'but just the same I can't help feeling we'd be safer to stick together. This west route is through some mighty bad country, I've been told. Salty outfits operating between here and Dodge City. I calc'late hardly any bunch would take the chance of tackling a big drive handled by nigh onto three hundred waddies, but when you bust 'em up this way and the individual herds have to bed down at night by themselves, well, that sort of makes for pickings by a smart and salty bunch.'

'Have you been over this west route before?' Slade asked.

'Nope,' Perkins replied, 'and I don't reckon many of the boys have, either. Goodwin insisted on it because it does cut off a good many miles, and he says the going is just as good as farther east.'

Slade nodded, and did not comment at the moment.

As a result of Goodwin's plan, it was well into the afternoon before the last herd, the Bradded L, crossed the Red. Goodwin's Scab Eight herd, far to the front, broke trail.

Walt Slade's face was thoughtful as he watched Lane Branton's cows take the water.

For now only the Bradded L herd, still by far the largest unit of the drive despite its five hundred-head loss, remained on the south bank of the Red.

'Let Branton's bunch get a good start before we cross,' he told Perkins. 'Things have cooled down a mite but there is still bad blood between the outfits. Some young swallerforker may get mixed up with another of the same sort and start a rukus, and a thing like that spreads mighty fast and can easily get out of control. We can't afford to have anybody put out of commission right now. We may need every hand we have before we reach Dodge City, and the same goes for Branton.'

'I can't understand why Pace didn't keep Branton up in front with him,' Perkins complained. 'Here Branton is following Tom Ward's outfit and we're following Branton. Things being as they are, it don't seem to make sense to me.'

'I thought of that, too,' Slade admitted 'but the trail boss is the trail boss, and on a drive what he says goes. Anyhow, we'll keep well to the rear of Branton and Ward.'

Not seeing any advantage in further worrying the old cowboy, Slade did not mention that the Bradded L, bringing up the rear of the drive, was in the most vulnerable spot so far as a possible raid by wideloopers was concerned. Against such a possibility he intended to take all precautions.

Once the cows were across the river, the herd was lined up in marching order and headed north by slightly west across the plains of Oklahoma. Nobody rode directly in front of the herd. Near the head of the marching column rode the point men to act as pilots, working in pairs. When a change of direction was desired they would ride abreast of the foremost cattle, one pulling away from the column, the other quietly veering toward it. The cattle would swerve away from the approaching horseman and toward the one receding from them. Picked hands were assigned to this post of great responsibility.

About a third of the way back behind the point men came the swing riders, where the herd began to bend in case of a change of course. Another third of the way back rode the flank riders, who assisted the swing riders in blocking any tendency on the part of the cows to sideways wandering, and to help drive off foreign cattle that might seek to join the herd.

'Keep your eyes on those hills to the west all the time,' Slade cautioned his men. 'A sudden charge out of a canyon and half of you will be on the ground before you know it, if you let the hellions get the jump on you. It's happened just that way on this western route; the devils will cut out a hundred prime head and be back in the hole before the swing and flank men can get back to help you, those of you still in shape to want help, which wouldn't be many. And try

66

to follow them into the gorge and you get blown from under your hat. They know every crack and crevice in the hills and the hidden trails that lead to New Mexico. So keep your eyes open and don't get caught settin'. I'll be back here every now and then and I don't want to find anybody asleep on the job.'

Having experienced nearly two weeks of the authority of the tall range boss, the driver riders made up their minds that nobody would be caught asleep.

'I'd as soon tangle with a mountain lion and give him first bite,' a tough old waddie observed to the accompaniment of a general nodding of agreement.

'Tom Ward says a lot of folks think *he* is an owlhoot,' remarked another.

'Maybe he is, and then again maybe he ain't,' replied the first speaker. 'Anyhow, no sheriff has ever thrown him in the calaboose. If he is an owlhoot, I figure he's one of the John Ringo sort, when handling an honest chore he handles it as an honest chore should be handled. El Halcon has that kind of a reputation, too, you know, so I reckon we ain't got anything to worry about except doing what he says the way he says it; he sure don't stand for no foolishness.'

'He's got another kind of reputation, too,' piped up a young hand. They say he's the singingest man in Texas; maybe we can get him to sing for us some night. I've heard that rattlesnakes and horned toads crawl out in the open and shed tears when El Halcon sings.'

Following the drag came the remuda—the spare horses—in charge of a wrangler. Last of all rumbled the big chuck wagon with the usually bad-tempered cook bounding around on the high seat, handling the reins and cursing everything and everybody with amazing fluency. Late in the afternoon, the wagon would skirt around the herd and get in the lead, so that the cook and his assistant might make camp in the place selected by the outfit's trail boss and have supper ready by the time the herd was bedded down.

Slade and Seth Perkins took up a position near the front of the herd but well to one side after the river was crossed. Ahead was rolling rangeland that extended to the east as far as the eye could reach. To the west, however, was a range of dark and rugged hills toward which the route slowly veered.

Walt Slade eyed those lowering hills with scant favor.

'I can't help but feel that Goodwin made a mistake in choosing this west route,' he said. 'It's shorter, granted, but the east route is a lot safer. This route is through mighty bad country. Those hills over to the west—from there the Indians used to raid in the old days, and there have been plenty of raids from them since the Indians were cleaned out or brought under control. It's a regular hole-in-the-wall country over there, and the hangout for plenty of gentlemen who prefer to do their riding in the hours between sunset and sunrise. The Cimarron crossing is called Doran's and there isn't a worse hole in all Oklahoma. The drives from farther east pass that way also and there are always a lot of off-color hellions hanging around there on the lookout for pickings.'

'You've been this way before, then?' Perkins asked.

'Yes,' Slade replied briefly. He did not choose to explain that the trip entailed the pursuit of a notorious outlaw and killer who had fled Texas, seeking sanctuary in those same dark hills to the west, and not finding it. Finding instead 'Trail's End' at the muzzles of El Halcon's flaming guns in hell-roaring Dodge City.

'You'll ride ahead and pick out the bedding places, I suppose?' said Perkins.

'Yes, I'll ride trail,' Slade answered, 'but I want you to ride about a mile behind me; you'll be able to spot me on all the rise crests. That way, if something should happen, you can hightail back and alert the hands.'

'You figure we might run into trouble?'

'I don't think we have anything much to worry about today or tomorrow,' Slade decided. 'But the day after we'll be skirting the base of those sags and be making camp smack up against them. Then we'll have to keep our eyes skinned.'

69

'Don't look like anybody would be plumb loco enough to tackle a big outfit like this,' Perkins remarked.

'And because we are a big outfit and because of the fact we could be lulled into a sense of false security, makes it imperative that we should be on the watch,' Slade replied. 'There are smart men hanging out in this section of the country and a smart man can sometimes figure out something that takes the unwary at a disadvantage. We'll hope there is no trouble awaiting us, but take every precaution against the possibility that there is. Don't forget, now, stay a mile or so behind but keep me in sight as much as you can.'

Slade forged ahead of the herd. He rode swiftly but missed no detail of his surroundings, shaking his head as he eyed the distant hills. They appeared uttterly devoid of life, but Slade knew that where they were concerned, appearances could be deceptive. It was logical to believe that the outlaws who hung out or travelled back and forth there must have been informed of the approach of the great drive which had been hung up so long on the south bank of the Red. And just as logical to believe they would be watchful for an opportunity to cut out a valuable herd and run it west to northern New Mexico or southern Colorado, where there was a ready market for stolen stock. Slade was taking no chances.

From the crest of a tall rise he spotted the dust cloud that marked the position of Lane Branton's marching herd. With satisfaction he noted that Branton had a full five mile lead on the Bradded L. He saw to it that the herd ahead still held that distance when he selected a bedding down spot; there would be scant chance of the two outfits getting together.

As Slade predicted, the day and the one following passed uneventfully. But the third day out from the Red found the Bradded L herd plodding in the shadow of the hills. The track was a deep depression a good hundred yards in width.

'An old buffalo trail,' Slade told Perkins. 'Beaten out by the bison travelling for centuries from one feeding ground to another. The bison were smart, smarter than plenty of ranchers who allow their pastures to be eaten down until they're worthless. The bison would graze over an area for only so long as the grass was strong and healthy. Then they would migrate to other pastures and later come back to their original feeding range after it had recovered and become luxuriant once more. Yes, it makes for easier going, all right; we should hit the Canadian by day after tomorrow, I'd say.'

'And I reckon it'll be full to the brim with water, too,' grunted the pessimistic Perkins.

'I doubt it,' Slade replied. 'If we can get by those hills okay I've a notion we'll have easy going till we reach the Cimarron. Then if we can get past Doran's Crossing without trouble we should be okay for the Arkansas and Dodge City.'

'Three more rivers to cross!' growled Perkins. 'Oh, well, maybe we'll make it. Anyhow, we don't have to worry about barbed wire fences and rows with the grangers over here.'

'Yes, that's an advantage,' Slade conceded. 'The farmers haven't gotten this far west yet. Also, there are no spreads jumpy over the danger of Spanish fever brought in by strange herds.'

'No tick fever on the Brazos,' Perkins reminded him.

'No, but it's sometimes hard to convince the Oklahoma and Kansas ranchers that there isn't,' Slade answered. 'They lump the Brazos, the Trinity and the Nueces together. They regard dubiously any herd from central or south Texas.'

CHAPTER NINE

All day long Slade watched the hills to the west with eyes that missed nothing. He noted the movements of birds on the wing or in the brush, observed with care the actions of little animals scurrying through the grass, especially if they happened to come from the west. But not once did he see anything to arouse suspicion or alarm.

However, instead of taking comfort from the fact he was beset with an added unease. If anybody was keeping tabs on the marching herd they were doing it so expertly as to avoid detection by even the eyes of El Halcon, which, folks were wont to maintain, could see around corners and through chunks of mountain.

What bothered Slade more was the possibility that the assumed outlaws in the hills were not following the progress of the herd but anticipated where it would bed down for the night and were making preparations accordingly. The daily progress of the drive was fairly uniform and the ground covered in a day's march could be pretty accurately anticipated. Also, bedding down spots were dependent on the proximity of the essential grass and water. The owlhoots, familiar with every foot of the ground, might figure correctly just where it would be forced to spend the night.

All mere conjecture, of course, but there was another factor Slade had learned not to ignore. In men who ride much alone down the years, especially those who follow the dim trails of outlaw land, there develops an uncanny sixth sense, an instinct that warns of peril where none, apparently, is present. And

73

all day the silent monitor in his brain had been setting up a noiseless but persistent clamor. Slade had a 'hunch' that something untoward was due to happen and he respected such hunches, senseless though they might seem. He was very much on the alert.

As evening drew near, Slade noted from a rise crest that the dust cloud some six or seven miles to the front, which marked the progress of Branton's herd, was settling. Which was a plain indication that Branton was bedding down for the night. A mile and a half or so farther on he came to a terrain that was ideal for bedding down. Which Branton had passed by out of consideration for the needs of the following Bradded L outfit. Such procedure was common trail practice and rigidly adhered to even if the two outfits in question were on the prod against each other. It was also an indication that there was no practical night spot between its location and where Branton had halted his herd.

The location was favorable for spending the night by all normal estimates. From a canyon that opened out of the hills to the west ran a fairly broad and deep stream. Its banks were clothed with a luxuriant growth of grass. The ground was flat and to the east the country was visible for miles.

But one feature did not recommend it to El Halcon. He did not like the looks of the narrow, brush-grown canyon whose gloomy

74

mouth was less than a couple of hundred yards distant. How far back into the hills it ran he had no way of knowing, perhaps all the way through the range, and he had not the slightest desire to explore its depths. If by any chance somebody was holed up in there awaiting the arrival of the herd, to do so would just be a convenient way to commit suicide.

However, without doubt, here was the only practical spot to spend the night. That is, unless he wished to go ahead and share a bedding ground with Branton's outfit, which he was decidedly loath to do. He resolved to utilize what he was practically forced to, but to take precautions.

So when the chuck wagon arrived, he ordered it across the creek and some little distance beyond the north wall of the canyon. The cook gave him a puzzled look but said nothing. The new range boss might be loco, but the cook was evidently of the opinion that it would be wiser not to argue, even though a rather long carry of pots, pans, provisions and Dutch ovens was entailed. He went to work on the evening meal.

Seth Perkins had arrived with the wagon. He joined Slade on the creek bank where the Ranger stood deep in thought. Slade nodded but did not speak. Perkins nodded back and waited; he had learned to respect those periods of silence; he merely looked expectant.

Slade gazed absently at the swiftly flowing

water at his feet. Suddenly, however, he leaned forward a little, his gaze concentrating on a tiny object that came bobbing along on the current.

'Seth,' he said, 'don't start or make any obvious move, but do you see it there on the crest of that ripple?'

'Why,' said Perkins, 'it's a cigarette butt.'

Even as he spoke, the little cyclinder dissolved into a scrap of waterlogged paper and a shower of tiny brown particles that swiftly sank.

'Yes, it was a cigarette butt, all right, what of it?' Perkins asked.

'Doesn't it strike you sort of funny that a butt should come floating along like that?' Slade asked.

'Why, yes,' Perkins admitted. 'Wonder how it got there?'

'The obvious answer is that somebody tossed it into the creek and no great distance up-stream, otherwise the paper would have become soaked and disintegrated before it reached here,' Slade replied.

'You mean you think somebody is up there somewhere?' Perkins asked.

'Don't turn your head,' Slade said sharply. 'I don't think that brain tablet rolled itself and crawled into the water,' he added dryly.

Perkins stared as understanding struck home. 'And you believe—' he began.

'I don't know exactly what to believe,' Slade

76

replied, 'but this I *know*—we're going to take every precaution against a possible raid tonight. There's somebody up that canyon, that's sure for certain. Could be only a harmless hunter or prospector, but I hold that doubtful. This is a perfect spot for a swift and daring raid against an unprepared outfit. They could swoop out of that crack and be all over us before we realized what was happening.'

'And cut out a couple of hundred and off with 'em!' Perkins growled.

'Or run off the whole herd, taking their time about it,' Slade added grimly.

'But—but we got thirty hands with us!' Perkins exclaimed.

'Thirty dead men would be no hindrance,' Slade said, even more grimly. 'Don't you see it, Seth? With only a couple of nighthawks riding herd and the rest of the outfit asleep around the fire, they could just about wipe us out with a single volley or two, and down everybody else before we could get into action. I have a feeling that not only has somebody designs on the herd but they're all set for mass murder as well. I may be wrong, although I don't think I am, but it's too serious a matter to take chances with. We'll get ready for business and if something is tried, we'll see if we can't turn the tables on the sidewinders. Don't say anything to the boys when they arrive; I don't want them acting nervous and casting glances toward that canyon. If somebody up there is keeping an eye on us, that would tell them we've caught on and they might try some method other than the one I think they contemplate. Just go along with the normal procedure of making camp and bedding down. As soon as it gets dark, we'll proceed to put our own little plan in action. Understand?'

'Uh-huh,' grunted Perkins, 'and I got a funny prickly feeling up and down my backbone. Suppose the hellions are up there just waiting for the rest of the bunch to show before they crack down?'

'We'll have to chance that,' Slade replied. 'I don't think there is any danger of it happening, though. Their logical course is to wait until they figure everybody but the night hawks is asleep. It wouldn't be good sense, from their point of view, to start a battle with the outfit scattered about and wide awake. I think we're safe from attack until around midnight. They'd take into consideration the fact that Branton's outfit is bedded down within possible gunshot hearing and would naturally prefer they'd be asleep, too, and not on the alert. They would hope for several hours start to Colorado before the rest of the drive realized what had happened.'

'And I hope *all* of Branton's bunch are at their bedding place,' Perkins observed with meaning.

'That'll be enough of that,' Slade told him.

Perkins didn't argue. 'Now I see why you

78

ran the chuck wagon so far across the creek,' he commented.

'Yes, that wagon is one of my chief worries,' Slade said. 'Miss Clara sleeps in it, you know. So I tried to place it as much out of the way of chance of flying lead as possible. I still don't feel good about it. Luckily, she usually retires to the wagon shortly after supper is over. I don't want her to catch on to what's in the wind.'

'She's a mighty smart girl, and I notice she always has her eyes on you,' Perkins remarked. 'Maybe she won't catch on, but I wouldn't bet on it.'

'I'm afraid you're right about that,' Slade concurred.

Since leaving the Red, Slade had been too fully occupied with his multitudinous duties to accord Clara Lake much attention. He had sensed that she was covertly studying him from time to time.

Nothing remarkable about that, however. He was in charge of the great shipping herd, the loss of which could be crippling to the owner. Naturally she was concerned about the man upon whom the responsibility of bringing the cattle safely to Dodge City rested. And it was logical to believe that she had learned something of El Halcon's dubious reputation. She might well be just a mite worried about her choice of a range and trail boss. Well, that could bide; right now he had troubles of his own.

Before the herd arrived, Slade carefully studied the terrain. He noted that the ground sloped up to the cliffs that walled the canyon mouth, with a narrow bench at their base. The bench was about fifteen feet above the level of the grassland where the herd would spread out to graze. The cook had his fire going near the creek bank and around that fire, the crew would lay out their bed rolls for sleep, less than a hundred yards from the canyon mouth.

It was ticklish work, moving about in the open with the chance that sharp eyes were watching their every move and not knowing what the possible outlaws might take into their heads to do. Perkins was plainly jumpy, although he masked his trepidation with an elaborate carelessness. El Halcon himself was not as comfortable as he could have been even though he did not anticipate possible trouble until well after nightfall.

The herd rolled in and the tired cows drank from the stream and then began to graze. The cowboys attended to their horses and finished other necessary chores and were ready to eat when the cook bellowed. Clara Lake sat with Slade and Perkins a little apart from the others. She was unusually silent and Slade felt that she was studying him more intently than usual. As the shadows began to thicken, however, she went to the wagon where her bed was laid out and disappeared inside it.

Slade heaved a sigh of relief. Very likely she would soon be asleep and as much out of harm's way as was possible under the circumstances.

It was the custom for the hands to smoke and yarn for an hour or so before rolling up in their blankets. The cook cleaned up and made necessary preparations for an early breakfast. Slade glanced toward the canyon mouth, which was now a huge rectangle of blackness.

'Let the fire die down,' he ordered. The hands glanced at him wonderingly but offered no comment. Slade waited until the flames had sunk to glowering embers, then swung into action. First he turned to the night hawks who were preparing for their lonely chore. He indicated three suits of spare overalls and shirts he had previously removed from the wagon.

'Stuff those things with grass, then rope them to the backs of three of the quietest horses of the remuda, horses that are accustomed to ambling around the herd without guidance,' he ordered. 'Don't waste time asking questions. I may be wrong, and I hope I am, but I'm afraid we won't get through this night without trouble. Now bundle the bed rolls to look like men sleeping around the fire. Then get up on that bench under the cliffs. If something does cut loose, we'll be in a position to handle it.'

'You figure some hellions may make a try

for some of our cows?' a young puncher asked as he and his companions busied themselves with the chores Slade had set them.

'I have a feeling that if they make a try, it will be for the whole herd,' Slade replied. 'And you know without me telling you what that would mean to a bunch pounding their ears around a dying campfire.'

Muttered oaths and ejaculations greeted the remark. The experienced hands didn't need to be told.

The men entrusted with the task of manufacturing and placing the dummies came stealing back through the shadows.

'We put hats on 'em,' one chuckled, 'and in the starlight they look perzactly like sleepy cowpokes, only more intelligent than most.'

A little later Slade stepped back from the glow of the dying fire and nodded his satisfaction. The cleverly arranged bedrolls simulated perfectly the forms of sleeping men.

'Now get the rigs on your horses and hobble them just this side of the chuck wagon,' he ordered. 'Maybe we'll get a chance for a finish job on the hellions.' He had already left Shadow ready for action save for the bit that could be flipped into his mouth in a moment of time. Satisfied that everything yas taken care of, he led the way to the shallow bench overlooking the camp and the canyon mouth. He spread out his men along in the shadow of the cliff, he himself taking the post nearest the canyon's mouth. The outfit settled down in silence to await developments.

Slade was leaning back comfortably against the cliff face and wishing he dared light a cigarette, when a figure stole toward him from the gloom. An instant later he recognized Clara Lake. Under his breath he swore an exasperated oath.

'What the devil are you doing here?' he demanded in an angry whisper.

Before replying she sat down beside him, stretching her slim, shapely legs out in front of her and settling herself against the cliff face in a manner that promised permanency.

'Expecting trouble, aren't you, Walt?' she asked softly.

'I'm taking precautions against possible trouble,' he answered. 'Why didn't you stay in the wagon where you belong, where you'll be at least a little safer if something does cut loose?'

Again she did not directly answer his question.

'I believe those are my cows down there, aren't they?' she said. 'And if something happens you'll be risking your life to keep me from losing them, won't you?'

'That's my job, isn't it?' he demanded in exasperation.

'Perhaps,' she conceded, 'but I don't consider it exactly ethical, pedantically speaking, for me to hole up in safety while you do so.'

'Ethics, the devil!' he retorted. 'Plain common sense should come before ethics, Miss Lake.'

'In a way it does, circumstances being what they are,' she countered. 'If something does happen, every gun will count, and I'm a pretty good shot, Mister Slade.'

'What I should do,' he sputtered wrathfully, 'is tuck you under my arm, carry you back to the wagon and put you in it.'

'If you try it, I'll make a noise,' she threatened, 'and I know you don't want any noise right now, *Mister* Slade.'

Walt Slade gave a hollow groan. 'Please, Clara,' he pleaded, 'it's going to be deadly dangerous up here if something does happen.'

'That's better, Walt?' she replied. 'But I'm going to stay right here with you; I want to stay. I'm sorry you don't want me.'

'Confound it! who said I didn't want you!' he exploded, if one can explode in a whisper. 'It's just that I'm worried about you.'

'That's nice!'

Slade gave up; he felt he was losing ground every time he opened his mouth.

'All right,' he said, 'you might as well come over here and be comfortable.' He reached out a long arm and drew her close. She snuggled her curly golden head against his shoulder and appeared perfectly content.

CHAPTER TEN

The starlight had brightened somewhat and from where he sat, Slade could dimly make out the rolled blankets beside the faintly glowing fire, and the forms of the three dummies that lurched and swayed on the backs of the trained horses pacing slowly around the bunched and sleeping herd. He could not see his companions in the deep shadow at the cliff base, and they made no sound.

Clara Lake was also silent, and so motionless that Slade believed she was asleep.

She wasn't, and it was not the amazingly keen hearing of El Halcon but a woman's intuition that gave the first warning.

'Walt,' she suddenly breathed, 'there's something moving back in that canyon; I feel it.'

Slade gazed toward the huge rectangle of blacker shadow that was the gorge mouth, and saw nothing. He strained his ears, and heard nothing. A moment later, however, he did catch a sound, a soft, stealthy sound, as if a giant were gently pressing back the branches of the tall growth with his hands.

The sound loudened a little, then Slade heard a tiny jingle, the movement of a bit iron as a horse tossed its head.

'Keep down,' he whispered to his companion.

85

'I believe they're coming out.'

She lifted her head from his shoulder and he sensed rather than saw her draw the gun that hung from the belt encircling her trim waist.

'Keep down!' he repeated urgently. 'They—'

The rest of his low-voiced mutter was drowned by a prodigious crackling and crashing. From the black canyon mouth bulged a compact body of shadowy horsemen charging straight for the camp. There was a roar of gunfire. Orange flashes stabbed the gloom. The dummies atop the horses lurched and swayed and the blanket rolls jerked and twitched as bullets hammered them.

'The snake-blooded devils!' Slade exclaimed as the riders on the flat below continued to slash the blanket rolls with bullets. He jerked both guns and let drive.

A horseman whirled from his saddle as the big Colts spoke. A ripple of fire ran along the edge of the bench and two more saddles were emptied. The triumphant whoops of the raiders changed to yells of alarm. They whirled their horses, shifted their aim. Bullets smacked against the cliff face. Others kicked up spurts of dust or showers of stone splinters. Along the bench sounded a yelp of pain and a bitter curse; somebody had caught one.

'For God's sake, Clara, keep down!' Slade yelled between shots. 'There's a score of devils and they're fighting back. Keep down! Hug the ground!'

There was no answer except the steady banging of the gun by his side.

The outlaws charged for the canyon mouth, but the withering fire from the bench drove them back. Slade saw two more fall, but a yell along the bench told him his own force was not escaping scathless.

On the ground below a deep voice bellowed an order. The outlaws scattered, darting in and out among the milling cattle, making for the canyon by ones and twos, shooting as they rode. A bullet grained the flesh of Slade's arm. He heard a little gasp beside him.

'You hit?' he called in an agony of fear.

'Just grazed my temple,' she panted. 'Look out, there come two more!'

Slade fired and one of the riders reeled in the saddle, clutching the horn for support; but both kept their seats and flashed into the canyon and out of sight. After them streamed others, leaning far over to present as small a target as possible and firing under their horses' necks, Indian style.

'There goes one across the prairie that couldn't get through the cows!' Clara shrilled.

Slade saw him, a tall man on a big dark-colored horse, a flickering motion in the starlight. He leaped to his feet, rushed down the slope and raced to where he had left Shadow. If he could run the fellow down he might be able to force him to talk and divulge valuable information. Flipping the bit into the big black's mouth, he swung into the saddle and sent Shadow charging in pursuit.

'After him!' yelled Seth Perkins. 'The hellion may lead him into an ambush!'

The cowboys, all that were able to walk, ran for their horses, Clara Lake with them. And it was she who was astride her splendid blue moros even before the agile Perkins had mounted.

A gibbous moon was rising in the east, casting a lurid light over the prairie and Slade had no difficulty keeping his quarry in view. However, almost immediately he was forced to slow Shadow; the going was bad, the ground rough and full of holes made by burrowing creatures. He was able to hold the distance but that was about all. The fugitive was within rifle shot but Slade decided to hold his fire and use the big Winchester only as a last resort. Perhaps he could get close enough to fan the other's face with a slug or two and possibly cause him to pull up. Or to send a bullet through his arm or shoulder. He earnestly desired to take the fellow alive.

Suddenly the horseman turned and Slade exclaimed aloud. His face was covered by a black mask.

'Shadow, that's the big skookum he-wolf of the pack, I'll bet money!' he ejaculated. 'Those other hellions weren't masked, I'll swear to that. *He* is mighty anxious to keep his face covered, which is interesting and may be important. Take it, horse, we've got to get him!'

Shadow was doing his best under the circumstances and the fugitive did not draw farther ahead. He stood out hard and clear against the sky as he topped a ridge, and when Shadow reached the crest he was still plainly visible, but no closer than before. They tore down the sag and drummed across the level. Ahead was another ridge with stars seeming to touch its crest like beads of flame strung on a silver wire. The fugitive's horse toiled up it to the summit, with Shadow just reaching the first swell of the slope.

And then it happened, the most dreaded accident of the rangeland; Shadow put a front foot in a badger hole. He surged back with all his strength to save his leg, and did so, but he was thrown off balance and fell, hurling Slade to the ground with stunning force.

The outlaw, glancing back, saw the mishap. He reined in on the crest, threw a rifle to his shoulder and took deliberate aim at the prostrate Ranger. The rifle cracked, but the light was not good, the distance considerable and the angle bad. The slug spurted dust a foot or so from Slade's face.

The outlaw fired again; this time the bullet struck closer. Another shot and he'd have the range. He steadied the rifle barrel, aimed carefully.

But before he could pull trigger, the following Bradded L hands surged over the opposite rise. A storm of bullets whizzed around him. He whirled his horse and fled into the darkness.

Cursing insanely, Seth Perkins sent his mount charging down the slope to where Slade lay, the others pounding behind him.

'The sidewinder got him!' a puncher bawled, and followed up with crackling oaths. Perkins jerked his horse to a sliding halt, but Clara Lake was on the ground before he was.

*   *   *

When Walt Slade regained full consciousness —he really never went completely under, but the force of the fall momentarily paralyzed his body—his head was pillowed in Clara's lap. Somebody had brought water from the stream and she was sponging his temples with it. He felt very comfortable right where he was, decided to stay there for a while and did. Suddenly, however, he remembered that Shadow also had taken a bad tumble. He sat up, Clara's arm solicitously about his shoulders, Perkins hovering over him.

'My horse?' he asked.

'He's okay,' Perkins reassured him. 'Limping a little on his left front foot but it's just a bruise and not bad; he can pack you, if you feel up to riding. Fell with you, eh?'

'That's right, and the hellion got away,' Slade replied.

'Yep, he got away,' said Perkins. 'Scooted down the far sag and we didn't follow him. Reckon it wouldn't have done us any good if we had; that was a mighty good horse he was forking. Seems to me I've seen a horse somewhere before with that sort of a running stride. I couldn't catch the color in this blasted yellow moon light, but I could almost swear I know that horse. You didn't get a look at the devil's face?'

'He was wearing a mask,' Slade answered.

'The devil he was!' grunted Perkins. 'I'd bet the others weren't. Something darn funny about all this. How you feeling?'

'I'm okay,' Slade stated. 'Just had all the breath knocked out of me and couldn't move for a while.'

He stood up, Clara still supporting him with a slender, rounded arm. He grinned down at her.

'Quite a night for you, little lady,' he chuckled, 'How do you like riding trail herd?'

'I love it,' she replied, and Slade believed she meant it.

They mounted and rode back to the camp. Three injured hands who had been left behind had gotten the cattle bunched and under control. One was cursing a bullet slashed arm, another was limping about on a punctured thigh, while the third was remarking pungently on much 'purtier' he was going to look with the scar that would be left by the slug that passed through his cheek.

Slade took a roll of bandage and some antiseptic ointment from his saddle pouch and expertly dressed the wounds, which he decided were of little consequence where such hardy individuals were concerned.

'We got seven of the sidewinders,' the puncher with the gashed cheek exulted. 'One of 'em wasn't quite gone when I got to him but he wouldn't talk and died cussin' me. Plenty salty, all right.'

The bodies had been laid out in a row on the creek bank. By the light of lanterns the cook broke out, Slade and Perkins examined them.

They were a pretty average looking lot, with nothing much distinguishing about them. Which did not surprise Slade, knowing as he did that there is no such thing as a criminal physiognomy: folks used to take John Welsey Hardin for a preacher. He wasn't.

Slade was examining the contents of the pockets and finding nothing of note aside from a good deal of money, when Perkins touched him on the arm. The old puncher was wearing a peculiar look.

'Walt,' he said in low tones, 'I've seen a couple of these jiggers before—the one with the broken nose and that one with the red birth mark on his cheek.'

'Where?' Slade asked.

'Down on the Brazos, in a saloon in Warton,' Perkins replied. 'I saw 'em more'n once, I'll swear to it. What the devil does it mean?'

'I'd say it means somebody trailed the Bradded L herd from the Brazos country,' Slade answered dryly.

'Or rode with the drive,' Perkins growled.

'Not impossible, but not necessarily with the particular herd of which you're thinking,' Slade said. 'You don't recall seeing either of them with the drive, do you?'

'No, I don't,' Perkins had to admit.

'I'd say it is highly unlikely that they accompanied the drive,' Slade said. 'Much more reasonable to believe they kept under cover and joined the rest of the bunch up here, after learning all they could of the drive's plans and progress. And it's not beyond the realm of probability that the whole bunch came from the Brazos. I seem to recall that an owlhoot or two have been seen down there at times.'

'You're darn right,' grunted Perkins. 'We've lost plenty of cows in the past year, and so have other spreads. Good market for wet cows over in Louisiana, almost as good as in Colorado or New Mexico.'

'A big bunch and knew their business,' Slade remarked musingly. 'They planned to take the whole herd and leave no witnesses.'

'And that would have been some haul, the

murdering skunks!' snorted Perkins. 'But we thinned 'em out a bit, anyhow.'

'Yes, but there's still a dozen or so left,' Slade pointed out, adding, 'And I'm of the opinion the one I chased is the leader of the pack and, very likely, the brains.'

'Wonder why he wore a mask when the others didn't?' pondered Perkins.

'Was very anxious that his face wouldn't be seen in case of an accident and one of us escaping is the obvious answer, I'd say,' Slade replied.

'And that means he's somebody we or some of us would know?'

'Presumably.'

Perkins started to say more, glanced at Slade and shut his lips. But there was little doubt in Slade's mind as to what he was thinking.

Slade suddenly raised his head. 'A horse coming this way, from the north, and coming fast,' he said.

Perkins made a dive for his rifle, which lay nearby.

'Hold it,' Slade cautioned. 'There's only one horse, and the rider's making no attempt at concealment. I'd say it's somebody from Branton's outfit who heard the shooting and decided to investigate.'

'And if he is, I aim to investigate him a bit if necessary,' Perkins growled.

Slade raised his voice to caution the others

as the beat of fast hoofs steadily loudened. A moment more and a man rode into the light of the fire that had been built up and was burning brightly. He was not one of Lane Branton's bunch but Slade recognized him instantly, as did the others.

It was Tom Ward.

The T Bar W owner's horse was lathered and both it and the rider were breathing hard.

'What happened here?' Ward burst out. 'I heard shooting.'

Perkins started to answer, but Slade quieted him with a gesture. He quietly explained the recent stirring events. As he spoke, Ward's eyes roamed over the camp, and they were anxious. Clara Lake stepped into the circle of firelight and Slade saw his chest heave mightily as he sighed with relief.

'Hello, Tom,' she greeted, cordially enough.

Ward ducked his head and muttered a reply. Slade forestalled the question he knew was rising to Seth Perkins' lips.

'You didn't hear the shooting clear up to your camp?' he asked.

Ward shook his head. 'No,' he replied, 'I was down at Branton's camp when I heard it. A gunshot carries a long ways on a still night like this and it's only about five miles to where he's bedded down. Branton wanted to come, too, but I told him he'd better stay right where he was.'

He grinned a little, and added, 'I figured

there was less chance of somebody taking a shot at me.'

Perkins' mouth tightened but Slade shot him a warning glance and he remained silent.

'Light off,' Slade invited. 'The cook's heating up coffee; reckon you could stand to share some with us.'

'I can,' Ward accepted gratefully. He dismounted and began rubbing down his horse, which still breathed heavily. Clara Lake walked over and joined him. Slade drew Perkins a little aside as the pair conversed together in low tones.

'Walt,' Perkins muttered, 'I don't believe that shooting could have been heard clean up to Branton's camp, even if it is a still night.'

Slade was wondering a little about that himself, but he cautioned Perkins to keep his own counsel.

'The contours of a section will sometimes do queer things with sounds,' he explained. 'Perhaps this range of hills, with cliffs all along here, acts as a sounding board and magnifies the echoes it casts back. I've seen just that happen in canyons.'

'Maybe,' Perkins grunted, 'but just the same I wish I'd got a better look at that horse the hellion you chased was riding. A jigger *could* circle around and come down from the north, you know.'

'Yes, he *could*,' Slade allowed, 'but so long as you have absolutely no proof that anybody did, don't go doing any loose talking about it.'

'Guess you're right,' granted Perkins, 'but I'm hanged if I don't wish I knew what the devil *is* going on.'

'You're not alone in that,' Slade said.

Tom Ward drank his coffee, made sure that his riding gear was okay and his horse fit to travel. Then he mounted and gathered up the reins.

'I'll be seeing you,' he told Slade. 'I'd better be getting back now; Branton will want to know what happened.' With a nod to Clara he rode north.

Clara Lake watched him go, and there was an inscrutable look in her blue eyes. Slade wondered if she were really interested in the personable young cattleman. She met his gaze and seemed to read his thoughts.

'I'm glad Lane didn't ride down here with Tom,' she said, and added, 'If one can't get the moon, one sometimes has to be satisfied with sixpence.'

Slade stared after her as she departed for the wagon. Usually fairly wise in the ways of women, he mistakenly wondered if she meant, convinced that Branton was beyond her reach because of his row with her father, she was willing to settle for Tom Ward.

The tired punchers went to sleep, but Slade sat on by the fire for some time, thinking deeply. He was very much of the opinion that the raids on the drive had their inception in the Brazos country and that he was up against a formidable opponent. He wondered if the person who masterminded the operations was riding with the drive, and had an uneasy premonition that he was.

The raids had been admirably planned and expertly carried out. The first had left two dead men behind, conceding that John Lake and Pete Rasdale had met their fate at the hands of the raiders. If the second had succeeded, the great Bradded L herd would have been driven off to the accompaniment of mass murder. Somebody was resourceful, daring and with an utter disregard for human life.

Slade couldn't help but feel that there was significance in the fact that both times the Bradded L had been singled out for a target. Of course, it could be but coincidence, but Slade didn't believe it was; with the drive consisting of thirteen herds, the law of averages appeared to deride such an assumption. The Bradded L, being the last in the line of march, was vulnerable, but it hadn't been the night of the storm. It looked like somebody was setting his sights for the Bradded L. Which paved the way for some interesting theories as to who and why.

Lane Branton, convinced that John Lake had wantonly depreciated the value of his property and had been responsible for his father's death, might be out to even up the score and at the same time accrue a neat profit for himself. Branton didn't strike Slade as the sort that would go in for wholesale slaughter, but he could be dominated by the cold killer, Cliff Hardy, who very likely would shoot a man with as little compunction as he would squash a fly.

And Tom Ward, for reasons of his own, might have thrown in with Branton. Slade did not doubt that he was really interested in Clara Lake. Seth Perkins had admitted that the loss of the big shipping herd would have put the Bradded L in precarious circumstances. Then Ward could come forward with a helping hand, which naturally would not hurt his chances with the girl who, it appeared, had always thought rather well of him.

Slade chuckled to himself as he reviewed the intricate web he had woven. The trouble was, there were too many loose threads banging around, with nothing substantial to which to anchor them. To mix figures of speech as thoroughly as his deductions, he was building on sand with drops of water. He gave up for the time being and joined the others in sleep.

CHAPTER ELEVEN

The following morning the herd continued its northern march. Slade thought it wise for the three wounded men to ride in the wagon for a day or two, but the individuals in question protested so vigorously that he rescinded the order with a grin.

'Why, I've cut myself worse than this shaving,' declared the man with a bullet hole through his cheek. 'Ouch! why do I always have to talk so darn much!'

About mid afternoon Slade discerned a horseman riding swiftly from the north. It turned out to be Pace Goodwin.

'One of Tom Ward's hands rode up to the head of the drive and told me what had happened,' he explained. 'I thought I'd better drop back and see if everything is okay.'

Slade assured him that everything was and Goodwin, with a nod, rode on for a word with Clara Lake.

A fine looking man, Slade thought, gazing after his broad back, and would very likely give Branton and Ward some competition for the favor of the winsome owner of the Bradded L.

Some little time later, when Slade was contemplating riding ahead to pick out a bedding-down spot, Goodwin reappeared and drew in alongside him.

Goodwin looked irritated, but Slade read a grudging respect in his fine dark eyes.

'I gather that your acumen and foresight prevented a catastrophe,' he observed.

'I merely took the precautions normal to a drive passing through hostile territory,' Slade deprecated.

'Perhaps, but it wasn't told to me exactly that way,' Goodwin returned dryly. 'Miss Lake is deeply grateful to you, and lavish in her praise.'

Slade suppressed a grin. He believed he understood Goodwin's irritation. Quite likely praise for another man from Clara Lake didn't set too well with the Scab Eight owner.

'Miss Lake is very kind,' he replied.

'Well, I guess she's got reason for thinking well of you,' Goodwin said. 'The loss of that herd would have been a serious matter for the Bradded L, to say nothing of the fact that her men, some of whom have known her ever since she was a baby, would have very probably been among the missing today.'

Slade merely nodded. Goodwin was also silent for a few moments, then abruptly he spoke, his brows drawing together in a frown.

'I have a suspicion, Slade, that somebody riding with this drive will bear watching,' he stated.

'Possibly,' Slade's voice was noncommittal. 'But who, and why?'

'Easier to ask than to answer,' Goodwin

retorted, adding with seeming irrelevance, 'Bad blood between outfits is sometimes responsible for strange things.'

Slade turned until his level gray gaze rested on the other's face.

'You are referring to the Triangle B and the T Bar W?' he asked.

'I did not mention names,' Goodwin protested. 'It would be presumptuous for me to do so. I merely referred to what is an obvious fact and commented on the possibilities inherent to such a condition.

'Look here, Slade,' he continued before the Ranger could speak, 'you must appreciate my position. I was elected trail boss of the drive by the owners. They hold me responsible for the safe arrival of the drive at Dodge City and you can't blame them for looking somewhat askance at me because of the things that have happened. A number of cattle have been stolen and two men murdered, one of them an owner. Last night there was another attempt that would very likely have been successful had it not been for your anticipating trouble and the way you handled the matter. If the Bradded L herd had been run off and the outfit murdered, the owners would have wondered, doubtless out loud, why I hadn't taken precautions to prevent such an occurrence.'

'It would hardly be logical for them to hold you responsible for something that happened twenty miles from your post in the drive,' Slade observed.

'Perhaps not,' Goodwin nodded, 'but under such circumstances you can hardly expect men to be logical. I'm trying to prevent something else of a like nature happening, and I can't afford to miss any bets. I am forced to consider that there *is* bad blood between certain outfits.

'Not that I hold the Bradded L altogether blame less,' he added. 'Perkins is provocative in the last degree.

He is firmly convinced that Lane Branton either killed John Lake or had him killed and has influenced others of his outfit to believe likewise. And Branton is just as convinced that Perkins and his bunch are out to kill him and had that intention even before the trail herd left the Brazos. I think that is why he hired Cliff Hardy as his range boss. And the way you, working for the Bradded L, handled Hardy must not have made him feel any better. So it is not beyond the realm of possibility that he has decided to strike first as the only way to prevent his own extinction; that's what worries me.'

Slade nodded without speaking; Goodwin's arguments were hard to refute and, from his viewpoint, he had presented the case admirably.

Goodwin's manner of speech interested Slade no little. It was that employed by one educated man when conversing with another.

He did not use a similar address toward the other members of the outfit. With them he was terse, colloquial. Which indicated, Slade thought, that he instinctively sensed that he, Slade, was no ordinary cowhand, or that he had knowledge to that effect. Which last *was* interesting.

Abruptly Goodwin voiced what Slade instantly felt he had been leading up to all the time.

'So it is just possible that last night's attack did not have the widelooping of the Bradded L herd as its objective,' he said.

'None of the men killed in the course of the attempt were Triangle B hands,' Slade pointed out.

'Of course not,' Goodwin replied, adding grimly, 'and Cliff Hardy was not connected with the Triangle B until recently. I understand that he ran with a rather bad bunch down in the Nueces country.'

The intimation was plain enough, but Slade decided not to discuss it further at the moment. Again he merely nodded.

'Well, I guess I'd better be getting back north,' Goodwin said. 'Hope you don't have any more trouble.'

He put spurs to his big bay and forged ahead at a fast clip. Slade allowed some little time to pass before he quickened his own pace in search of a suitable bedding down spot for the night. Glancing back after a bit, he spotted

Seth Perkins drifting along in his rear a mile or so behind. He rode on, the concentration furrow deep between his black brows.

The conversation with Goodwin had been somewhat disquieting. Lane Branton, believing his own life was in danger, might have resolved that his only chance for survival lay in striking the first blow. Unexpected attacks from ambush were not uncommon to rangeland feuds which were often conducted in a ruthless manner. And Tom Ward's appearance soon after the conclusion of the fight by the canyon mouth provided an interesting angle. It was not impossible, of course, that the shooting had been heard at Branton's camp, even though the distance was great for sounds to travel even on a still night. Seth Perkins, Slade knew, didn't believe any such thing. A like opinion was held by others of the Bradded L hands.

'It's a mess, all right,' he told Shadow, 'and we seem to be getting nowhere fast.'

That night the bedding down spot was well out in the open and there was no danger of a repetition of the experience of the night before. The herd rolled on again with the first light.

'We're away from the hills now and nothing much to worry about where cow thieves are concerned,' Slade told Perkins.

'Maybe not, but I'll bet we find something else to worry about before we make '

Dodge,' Perkins predicted pessimistically; and he wasn't wrong.

The Canadian crossing was negotiated without difficulty, but things looked different when they reached the Cimarron. The river was rising and already uncomfortably high.

'And a lot higher than it was when the first bunch went across, I'll bet money on that,' Perkins growled. 'The tail end of this infernal drive is catching it from every direction. Think we can make it across?'

'If we don't, we'll be stuck just like we were on the south bank of the Red,' Slade answered; 'but I think we can do it. We'll soon find out.'

Accompanied by several selected hands, Slade and Perkins headed across. The horses had to swim some but they reached the north bank without mishap.

'Yes, I believe we can do it,' Slade said. He waved his hand for the herd to come along.

Urged on by the hands, the cows took the water, streaking across the muddy torrent like exploding brown skyrockets, horns clashing, eyes rolling wildly. They climbed the opposite bank, shook off showers of glittering drops and immediately started grazing. Some were swept away by the current, as is always the case, but ot many; it was a highly successful crossing.

Next came the chuck wagon, a couple of big on wood logs lashed to each to help it With cowboys straining on ropes tied hard and fast to saddlehorns, others standing on the upstream side of the clumsy vehicle to keep it from overturning, it also made the crossing safely and rolled up the bank to the accompaniment of appalling profanity on the part of the cook, who had gotten his feet wet and was blaming all and sundry.

The remuda and the wranglers followed, with some of the drag riders who had held back to combat a possible emergency. Seth Perkins suddenly let out an exasperated oath.

'Look!' he snorted. 'There's Miss Clara riding across! Why the devil didn't she stay in the wagon where she was safe?'

Slade watched the girl anxiously, although he was not particularly apprehensive of her safety; the crossing was really not a very bad one for a skillful rider and it was unlikely that she would come to harm.

But the Cimarron is always bad, and unpredictable. Its bed is full of treacherous quicksands which can engulf a horse and rider, and there are holes where they are least looked for. During high water, sand is whipped up from the bottom and makes swimming difficult.

It appeared the blonde girl would reach the north bank without difficulty, when the unexpected happened. A great tree, loosened from where it had been wedged in the mud during low water, suddenly surged to the surface as a big fish leaps. The current caught it and sent it hurtling straight for the rider and her frantically swimming horse, slowly revolving, flailing branches whipping the water to foam.

'Good God! it'll get her!' howled Perkins.

Slade sent Shadow racing downstream. He loosened his sixty-foot rope, built a tight loop. Like a leaping beast of prey, the tree surged toward the doomed horse and rider. It struck. The horse was thrown free but the girl vanished from the sight of the horrified watchers on the bank.

Over rolled the tree, and suddenly the sun glinted on golden hair.

'She's tangled in the branches!' Perkins screamed. 'Oh, my God!'

From the back of the racing horse, Slade made his cast. It was a long throw for even the powerful arm of El Halcon, but the tight loop settled straight and true over the thick projecting stub of a broken branch. Shadow surged back on splayed hoofs. The rope hummed as the slack took up. But even Shadow's mighty strength, that could readily bust a fifteen hundred pound steer, could not match the Cimarron's resistless current. Slipping, sliding, clawing, he was dragged forward, snorting with anger, fighting for every inch of ground.

He couldn't halt the tree's progress, but he did stop the slow turning while the girl was still above water.

Slade leaped from the saddle, shucking off his gun belts, casting aside his hat. He stormed through the shallows and struck out for the tree with strong strokes. Thanks to Shadow's slowing its progress, he made it, forcing his way through the thrashing branches till he was almost within arm's reach of the prisoned girl.

With a twang like a giant harp string, the overburdened rope broke. Shadow fell backward. The slow turning motion resumed. Slade fought frantically to reach the girl, but he knew he was fighting a losing battle; another moment and they would both be submerged.

'They're both done for!' Perkins yelled.

A horseman swept past him charging down stream, rope in hand. Again a swift, accurate cast. Again a tightening twine staying for an instant the deadly revolving motion. The rider's horse slipped and floundered, but that moment's respite was all Slade needed. His long arm encircled the girl's waist and he tore her free, surging backward through the water.

A flailing branch swept both beneath the water, but Slade fought his way to the surface. Clara was gasping, gulping and half drowned, but she was conscious and knew what she was doing.

'Hands on my shoulders!' Slade told her. 'Don't put your arms around my neck and choke me.'

'I won't,' she sputtered cooly, if one can

sputter and still sound cool.

On the bank the roper held on for another agonizing second, curbing the progress of the tree till the swimming pair had fought free from the web of branches. Then his horse fell, hurling him to the ground. He lurched erect, flipped loose his twine and staggered down stream.

'Holy hoptoads! It's Tom Ward!' bellowed Perkins.

The current was swift, but Slade swam with long, strong strokes. Very quickly he was on his feet and floundering through the shallows, the girl cradled in his arms.

'May I put them around now?' she asked, and proceeded to do so before granted permission.

The Bradded L hands came streaming down the bank, whooping and yipping, to surround the rescued pair.

'Where's the man who threw that rope?' Slade asked as soon as he'd gotten his breath back.

A dozen pair of hands thrust Tom Ward to the front. Ward's face was white and strained, his eyes wild. He stared at Slade, drew a long and shuddering breath.

'Feller, you're a man to ride the river with!' he said thickly.

'Thank you,' Slade acknowledged the highest compliment the rangeland can pay, 'but if it wasn't for your quick thinking and

110

fine roping, I've a notion it would have been my last ride. And Miss Lake's, too,' he added. 'How'd you happen along at just the right time?'

'I had a hunch that maybe things mightn't go right down here when you hit the water, with the river rising like it was,' Ward explained. 'So when we crossed, I held back a bit and saw what was happening.'

'I'm darned glad you played that hunch,' Slade told him. 'Come on, we'll bed down here and have something to eat and some hot coffee.'

'Sorry, but I'd better be getting back to my outfit,' Ward declined. He gazed at Clara Lake for a moment, strode to his horse, which had regained its feet, and rode off.

'And that's a man to ride the river or anything else with,' Slade declared. He turned to Seth Perkins.

'Well?' he asked softly.

Perkins batted his hat over one eye, glowered, mumbled under his breath,

'I'm darned if I know!' he replied.

CHAPTER TWELVE

Clara Lake seemed perfectly content remain where she was, but Slade set her on feet.

'Trot along and get into dry clothes, you're shivering,' he told her. 'I see your horse made it to shore okay. Trot along, I'll take care of him.'

'She minds you like a pet cayuse, and she never would mind anybody else,' Perkins chuckled as the girl headed for the wagon, thoroughly drenched and bedraggled but still charming.

Slade chuckled, too, accepted his gun belts and hat from somebody who had retrieved them, emptied the water from his boots and hunted up Shadow, who wore a decidedly disgusted look but was none the worse for wear.

'Guess most of the credit is due you and Tom Ward,' Slade told him. 'If it wasn't for you two, we'd both have taken the Big Jump.'

Slade got into dry clothes while the herd was bedded down earlier than usual. But the grass was good, there was plenty of water available and the site was on a stretch of open prairie, so Slade thought that the few miles of progress lost were offset by the obvious advantages. After a good meal and plenty of hot coffee he felt fully recovered from the hectic activity of the afternoon.

After supper, the hands sat about the fire 'arning or playing cards. Slade walked along e river bank alone and stood watching silver bow of the moon reflected in the ulent water. And as on the night of the attempted widelooping, a slender figure stole out of the shadows and paused beside him.

'Well?' she said.

'Well,' he answered, 'you'd very likely prevent a lot of trouble by making up your mind one way or another.'

'Oh, I've made up my mind, but I'm afraid it won't do me much good,' she said.

'Tom Ward worships the ground you walk on,' he observed.

'Perhaps,' she conceded, 'but after thinking it over, if I can't have the moon, I don't believe I'll be content to settle for sixpence.'

'Now what do you mean by that?' he demanded.

She shrugged daintily. 'The Sybil has spoken, sir, you find the answer,' she replied.

Slade regarded her in silence for a moment, wishing he could see her expression better. Her face, he thought, was like a flower in the illusive glow of the moonlight.

'All right,' he said suddenly, 'I will.' He reached out, gathered her close. She raised her face to his and their lips met.

For a lingering moment she clung to him; then she drew back as far as the circle of his arms would permit.

'Well, did you find your answer?' she asked softly.

'Yes, I think I did,' he said, 'and I also think you are not being very wise, concentrating on a

113

man whose reputation is dubious, to put it mildly.'

The big eyes suddenly blazed. 'Oh, the devil!' she exploded. 'You may fool the boys, and some others, but you're not fooling me a bit. I know perfectly well what you are and why you're here.'

'Why am I here?' he asked, ignoring the first statement.

'To find out who murdered my father and bring him to justice.'

'Guesswork, or woman's intuition?'

'A combination of both, plus a rather intensive study of you during the past couple of weeks and more.'

Slade nodded, but did not further commit himself. She continued to regard him.

'Walt,' she asked, 'do you believe Tom Ward killed my father?'

'Nope.'

'How about Lane Branton?'

'I don't know,' he admitted frankly.

The girl shuddered. 'I'd hate to think such a thing of Lane,' she said. 'I know he has a violent temper—and so had Dad. I could understand he and Dad getting into a furious argument that ended in a shooting, but from what I have been told, I gather it was cold-blooded murder.'

'There is no proof that it was,' Slade pointed out. 'It could have happened just as you mentioned. Working on the premise that

114

Lane Branton was the man responsible for your father's death, and not conceding or even intimating that he *was* responsible, they could have met in the gloom of the approaching storm and gotten into an argument, with Branton or Hardy making the faster draw.'

'But how about the powder burns on Dad's shirt, and on poor Pete's, too?'

'Could mean either of two things,' Slade replied. 'Could mean that your father was killed by somebody he trusted and had no reason to fear, somebody who could approach close enough to shove the gun against his breast. But it could also mean that he and his adversary were standing close together in furious argument, as angry men will do—I've seen it happen just that way. Either supposition is plausible, you see.'

Clara shuddered. 'Walt,' she said slowly, 'doesn't it occur to you that you yourself may well be in terrible danger?'

It was Slade's turn to shrug. 'The danger can bide,' he replied lightly. 'I've become rather accustomed to it during the past few years.'

'But you'll be careful, for—my sake?'

'An excellent reason for me to be as careful as I can,' he answered.

She smiled wanly, and even in the moonlight he could see the red lips tremble a little.

'Can I consider that something in the way of

115

a promise?' she said.

'As much of a promise as can be given by a man who rides a lone trail and a long trail.'

'There is never a trail so long but that it turns, somewhere.'

'I'm considering that, very seriously,' he admitted. 'But come along, it's getting chilly out here. I'll take you back to the wagon.'

'And tuck me in?'

Slade chuckled. 'That could very easily lead to complications I'm not ready to face until I'm sure you know your own mind.'

'I know it,' she declared.

'Yes, under a moon like that one, but how about in prosaic daylight?'

'I know it, now and ever after; I'm not going to change.'

'Would look nice, wouldn't it, a rich woman with a wandering rider for a husband,' he teased.

'Then she really would be rich,' Clara retorted.

Slade laughed aloud. 'Trading repartee with you is a risky business,' he chuckled. 'Come on, now, it's time you were in bed.'

At the wagon he kissed her goodnight and returned to the river to ponder the problem that confronted him.

But his thoughts kept getting tangled with hair like spun gold and eyes the color of the Texas bluebells in the sun. Finally he gave up and went to see how Shadow was making out.

116

'Horse,' he confided to the big black, 'this may be it. I don't know for sure, but it may be. Think you can put up with a rival?'

Shadow did not deign to reply, and his expression was enigmatical.

The night passed without incident and with the first light the herd was on the move.

'What's them shacks up there?' Perkins asked, gesturing to a huddle of structures about a mile upstream.

'That,' replied Slade, a trifle grimly, 'is why we crossed down here instead of farther up where the water is a bit shallower. This is Doran's Crossing, you know, and that is Doran, from which the crossing took its name. The big building sprawled all over the flat is a saloon and is called Old Jane's Deadfall. An old harridan named Jane Doran first opened it up. She died or pulled out, I don't recall which, and the place passed on to as ornery a bunch of rapscallions as you'd hope not to meet in a long month's ride.'

'Plumb snake-blooded, eh?'

'A mild descriptive term. A respectable snake would be shocked to meet his mother in there. I didn't want the boys mixed up with that hell-hole, and I've a notion Goodwin had the same notion; he kept right on rolling. If they want to stop on the way back for a mite of questionable diversion, we'll have to let them, of course, but not until we get these cows off our hands.'

Perkins nodded agreement. 'One more river to cross, eh?' he observed.

'Yes, the Arkansas,' Slade said. 'I doubt if we'll have any trouble with the Arkansas, and right across is Dodge City, where anybody can easily have trouble if he doesn't watch his step.'

'Trouble ain't hard to find anywhere if you go looking for it,' Perkins observed sagely, adding, 'And sometimes you don't even have to look.'

'Precisely,' Slade concurred. 'Let's get moving. Four more days of easy going should see us across the Arkansas and safe in Dodge City.'

'From what I've heard of it, there ain't nobody safe there,' Perkins grumbled pessimistically. 'Oh, well, I've gotten so used to walking a tight rope between here and what they say is a better world, of late, that nothing bothers me much any more.'

'When your number isn't up, nobody can put it up,' Slade consoled him.

'Fine! If I could just know for sure when it isn't up,' Perkins acceded dubiously. 'Well, here's hoping.'

'I doubt if we'll even have to cross the Arkansas,' Slade observed. 'Usually the herds bed down on the south bank of the river and the buyers come across the toll bridge to look them over and bid.'

'I'm pretty sure John Lake made

arrangements with a buyer before we left the Brazos,' Perkins said. 'He always did do that,'

'Which will be an advantage,' Slade nodded. 'Then we'll have the cows off our hands sooner.'

The great trail herd pounded on across the plains of Kansas, with no untoward incident to mar the pleasant monotony of sun and moon and silver stars. Slade was not far off in his estimate and noon of the fourth day found them on the south bank of the Arkansas, which was low.

On the north bank of the river was the seething town that had for years been the cowboy capital of the north.

Dodge was not what it was when the steady stream of herds rolled up from Texas in endless succession, but it was still plenty lively, although Wyatt Earp, the famous frontier marshal, had cleaned it up a bit a few years before. There was even now little law in Dodge City, most of what there was, the law of the gun and the knife. Soldiers from the fort, mule skinners, bullwhackers, the remnant of the buffalo hunters and cowhands gathered there with all the peace and tranquillity of cats and coyotes living in a rattlesnake den. Anything could happen in Hell-roarin' Dodge, and usually did.

The cows were held in close herd on the south bank, the Bradded L some distance from the others. The owners crossed the toll bridge to make deals with buyers.

All except the Bradded L. As Perkins predicted, canny old John Lake had made his arrangements before leaving the Brazos. The representative of an eastern packing house was already on hand to do business. Two alert gents armed with sixguns and rifles accompanied him. Lashed to his saddle bow was a bulky satchel. He introduced himself to Clara and Slade, produced his credentials and wasted no time. He went over the tally sheets, examined the beefs with care and checked the tally. Then with pencil and pad he made his estimate and passed the result to Clara. Without even looking at the figures she handed it to Slade who conferred with Perkins and did a little figuring of his own.

'Okay,' he told the girl. 'A fair price.'

'Whatever you say must be right, Walt,' she said. The buyer, a shrewd old gent with considerable experience with the ways of the world glanced at her with an amused expression. He transferred his glance to Slade and nodded his approval. Chuckling under his mustache, he opened the satchel and began hauling out rolls of gold pieces, removing the bank's paper wrappings and verifying the count. Evidently addicted to orderliness, he carefully re-wrapped each roll after the sum was jotted down.

'Guess that makes it, Ma'am,' he said, transferring a few left over rolls to his pockets.

He shook the empty satchel. 'You can have the sack to pack it in,' he added. 'My boys will be here pronto to take over and run 'em across. A fine bunch of beefs and I'm glad to get 'em. Mighty sorry to hear the bad news about your father. I knew John Lake for years and it was always a pleasure to deal with him. So long, big feller,' he said to Slade. 'Been nice to meet you, and,' he added with a chuckle and a twinkle of his eyes at Clara, 'I got a sort of hunch I'll be seeing you again, when the next Bradded L herd rolls north. Although maybe this is the last one. If that's so, I'll be down Texas way and see you both. Goodbye, Ma'am, you sure got a nice color in your cheeks today.'

He rode off chuckling.

CHAPTER THIRTEEN

Seth Perkins didn't chuckle; he shook his head and his lined face wore a worried expression.

'I'll be glad when we're back in Texas,' he grumbled. 'That's a hefty passel of *dinero* to be packing around through outlaw country.'

That also was the opinion of Pace Goodwin when he rode up to the wagon a few minutes later.

'But we'll all be riding back together and I reckon the money we carry with us will be safe enough,' he added reassuringly. 'Well, Clara,

121

are you ready to cross the bridge? The boys will want a few days in town, of course, and I imagine you could use more comfortable quarters while we're here. The Wright House on Second Avenue is as good as any and quieter than most.'

Clara glanced inquiringly at Slade, who nodded slightly. 'All right, Pace,' she said, 'I'll be ready to ride in ten minutes.'

Less than an hour later the buyer's cowhands streamed into camp to take over the herd. They were experts and without delay they put the herd to the river. Quickly the broad stream was crowded with shaggy heads streaking through the tawny water like horned meteors across a yellow sky.

Slade watched them go and experienced a sense of satisfaction and relief. No matter what else might happen, he had brought the Bradded L herd through successfully. Now the cows were no longer his worry. But he had other things to think about.

Relieved of their charges and without a care in the world, the Bradded L punchers clattered across the toll bridge to seek diversion in Dodge City, chiefly south of the railroad tracks, where everything was wide open. However, Slade kept two of his older and most trusted hands to keep an eye on the chuck wagon and its valuable cargo.

'Be on your toes,' he admonished them. 'No telling what might cut loose.'

122

He drew Seth Perkins aside. 'I've got a chore for you,' he told the old puncher. 'I want you to keep Lane Branton and his bunch in sight all the time this evening. Branton brought a buyer back with him a little while ago and I figure he'll dispose of his herd in a hurry and head for town with his men. Don't get into a row with them. If you do, you'll very likely get yourself killed, and if that doesn't happen you'll answer to me personally for starting a rukus after I warned you not to. Don't forget, now, keep an eye on Branton and his bunch and don't let them get out of your sight.'

'I won't,' Perkins promised grimly. 'I got a score to settle with those horned toads and I'll do my part for a chance to get at them. Don't worry, I'll obey orders and keep in the clear.'

'Okay,' Slade nodded. 'I'll be seeing you before the night is over.'

Perkins rode off. Slade repaired to the chuck wagon and for some time was very busy under the canvas top. Finally he reappeared, batting white dust from his hands.

A little later he also rode across the bridge.

Slade did not enter one of the many saloons. Instead, he visited a hardware store and made a purchase that caused the old clerk who served him to blink in astonishment.

'Now what in blazes do you suppose that big cowboy wanted with all those things?' the clerk asked the proprietor after Slade had departed.

'Hard to tell,' answered the storekeeper. 'Texas cowhands are all crazy. Maybe he wants to use the holes for doughnut centers.'

The clerk snorted and ambled to the back of the store.

* * *

After leaving the store, Slade rode straight back to the Bradded L camp, in his saddle pouch a paper wrapped package that clanked to the motion of his horse. Again he entered the chuck wagon and again he was busy there for some time.

The old punchers had kindled a fire and were making coffee. Slade shared a steaming cup with them and then for the third time rode across the bridge.

'You know, Chuck, I've a notion he figures there's something off-color in the wind,' Bob Purdy remarked to his companion. 'He's busy as a mouse on a hot skillet.'

Chuck shrugged his scrawny shoulders. 'Could be,' he conceded. 'Anything liable to happen in this darned neck of the woods. Well, if it does, we'll be ready for it. The way he's riding back and forth across that bridge, he'll go busted paying toll.'

Crossing the bridge, Slade reached Bridge Street, or Second Avenue, and continued north to Front Street, the principal thoroughfare. For two blocks each way, Front Street widened into the Plaza, with business establishments lining the north side of the square. Two blocks east of Second Avenue was the famous Dodge House kept by Deacon Cox. It was situated at the north-east corner of the Plaza, the juncture of Front Street and Railroad Avenue. Wright and Beverly's store, for some time the most important commercial establishment of the Plains, was at the Second Avenue four-corners. Farther along toward First Avenue were the Delmonico Restaurant, the Long Branch Saloon, where the famous Luke Short ran the gambling, and still farther on the Alamo Saloon, the Alhambra Saloon and the popular hotel, the Wright House.

In this, the principal business section, there was something resembling law and order, but south of the railroad tracks most anything went. And it was south of the railroad, between the tracks and the Arkansas River, in Hell's Half Acre, that the visiting cowhands for the most part sought their diversion. Saloons, hurdy-gurdy houses, brothels and the worst of the gambling houses did a roaring business.

Slade wandered about the town for the remainder of the afternoon and evening. As the dusk spread its blue veil over the prairie, he obtained a bountiful helping of oats and a rubdown for Shadow at a livery stable.

'I'll be back for him in an hour,' he told the keeper and repaired to a nearby restaurant to enjoy a leisurely dinner.

At the Bradded L camp, the two old cowboys, Purdy and Martin, squatted beside their dying fire and smoked and yarned. They sprang to their feet with startled ejaculations as a tall figure loomed from the gloom.

'Oh, it's you, Slade!' exclaimed Purdy. 'How'd you slip up on us like that without us hearing you? You gave us quite a start— thought maybe you were somebody else.'

'If I had been somebody else, you would have very likely gotten a start—into the next world,' Slade told them grimly. 'Spread that fire out a bit so it'll die down faster.'

'You figure somebody might make a try for the money?' Martin asked nervously.

'I don't know,' Slade admitted, 'but I'm taking precautions against such a possibility.' He rolled a cigarette and sat down to wait for the glowing embers to coat with gray ash. His companions fidgeted uncomfortably, staring into the darkness, their hands close to their holsters. Slade remained calm and smoked with apparent relish. Finally he pinched out the butt and stood up, glancing about.

'All right,' he said. 'If there's anybody watching over by the bridge, I don't think they can spot us now or see where we're going. Come along.'

He led the way to a thin straggle of brush

that grew less than a score of yards from the site of the camp. Under the branches the darkness was intense, but where the wagon stood in the open, the wan sheen of the starlight dimly illumed objects.

The three took up their stand in the edge of the growth and waited. A tedious hour passed, and the best part of another, and nothing happened. Then abruptly Slade's keen ears caught a sound not heard by the others—the soft chuk of horses' hoofs on the thick grass, drawing slowly but steadily nearer. The sound ceased and the silence was intense, then broken by a faint popping of saddle leather. Slade laid a warning hand on his companions shoulders.

Another period of silence followed, then shadowy figures stole from the gloom and converged on the wagon. The starlight glinted on their drawn guns.

The raiders approached the wagon very cautiously, hesitated, came on again, apparently at a loss as to the whereabouts of the two guards. They paused for a second time and stood motionless in an attitude of listening, then resumed the slow advance. Reassured by the utter silence and lack of movement, they quickened their pace a little until they were within arm's reach of the vehicle.

Again the hesitant attitude of listening. Two detached from the group, glided to the rear of the wagon, paused once more.

'I slipped,' Slade breathed to his companions. 'I figured they'd just send two or three to crawl up and grab off the stuff; there's nearly a dozen of them. Well, we'll do what we can. Hunker down and stay put.'

He slid away from the others to pause several paces distant. A tiny glow filtered through a chink in the canvas as a match was struck inside the wagon.

The light flickered out; the pair reappeared, dropped to the ground. The others bunched around them. Slade drew both guns; his voice rang out, shattering the silence like a thunderclap.

'Elevate! you're covered!' he shouted, and glided back toward where Martin and Purdy hunkered low in the brush.

The raiders whirled to stare in the direction of his voice. For a moment they seemed stunned by the unexpected challenge. Then there was a flicker of movement, a gun blazed and a slug tore through the growth where Slade had stood an instant before.

Slade began shooting with both hands. Purdy and Martin started banging away as fast as they could pull trigger. A man fell. Another slumped beside him. A third whirled round and round and crumpled up like a sack of old clothes. Answering bullets slashed the growth. One burned a stinging streak along Slade's ribs. Another turned his hat sideways on his head. Purdy swore as still another nicked his shoulder, and fired the faster.

A fourth raider pitched forward to lie motionless. The others, with yells and curses, dashed into the darkness and disappeared. Slade tensed to race to where he had left Shadow, then relaxed. To pursue that number of desperate men through the darkness would very likely be fatal. He strained his ears to listen and again heard the soft patter of hoofs fading swiftly to silence.

'They're gone,' he told his companions, and began reloading his empty guns.

'But they got the money!' howled Purdy, dancing with impotent rage. 'I saw one of the hellions pack off the satchel!'

'Nope, they didn't get any money,' Slade replied cheerfully. 'They just got a bag of rolls of iron washers wrapped in the bank's paper. There'll be some tall cussing when that satchel is opened and its contents examined closely.'

'Well, I'll be hanged!' sputtered Purdy. 'But where's the *dinero*?'

'Safe in the bottom of the flour bin,' Slade told him. 'Let's see what we bagged.'

From where the remaining herds were bunched came the sound of shouts followed by a thudding of hoofs as the alarmed night hawks rose to find out what the devil was going on. Slade waited a moment, then again raised his voice.

'Come on in,' he shouted. 'Everything's

under control.'

The cowboys stormed up to the wagon, volleying questions, jerking their horses to a slithering halt.

'Some sidewinders tried to lift our herd money, that's what,' Purdy told them. 'But Slade outsmarted the hydrophobia skunks and we downed some of 'em. Get a lantern outa the wagon, Chuck, and let's look 'em over. Some of you fellers get the fire going again and put on the coffee pot; I need some.'

By the glow of the lantern and the rising flames of the fire, the dead raiders were hauled into view and examined. In Slade's opinion, they were about on a par with the seven that were killed when the abortive raid on the Bradded L herd was attempted many miles to the south, with nothing particularly outstanding about any of them.

'But I've seen a couple of 'em before, this thin one and the short one with red hair—down in the Brazos country—I'll bet money on it,' a Rafter H cowboy declared. 'They used to ride into Warton and drink there—I know I ain't mistaken. Yes, I saw 'em. Did the hellions trail us way up here?'

'Well, they're here,' said a companion, 'and here to stay.'

A shout sounded from the darkness nearby. 'I found a horse!' bawled another hand. He led the animal into the light, a good looking critter, saddled and bridled.

'Turkey Track,' somebody read the brand. 'Ain't that a southwest Texas outfit?'

'Gaines County, I think,' Slade said. 'Means nothing, though; horses can be sold, stolen, or strayed, and end up a long ways from where they were foaled.'

The others nodded assent.

'This one sure got a long ways from home,' remarked the burn reader.

'See if you can find the others,' Slade suggested. 'Maybe some more didn't follow the bunch as they rode off. That's a pretty fair looking cayuse, and a good rig for somebody. Finders keepers.'

However, no more horses were discovered. Slade had a cup of coffee with the others and prepared to ride to town.

'Stay inside the wagon and keep your eyes and ears open,' was his parting injuction to Purdy and Martin. 'I don't think there's much danger of further trouble tonight, but don't take chances.'

Several of the night hawks immediately volunteered to stay and help keep watch. Slade offered no objection and crossed the river to Dodge.

CHAPTER FOURTEEN

After considerable wandering about Hell's Half Acre, Slade found Perkins loitering in front of the Lone Star Saloon.

'They're in there,' the old puncher said, jerking his thumb toward the glowing plate glass. 'Branton and Ward and their outfits. Been there all evening—ain't never come out. Everything okay at the camp?'

Slade tersely related the details of what had happened. Perkins swore sulphurously.

'What the devil's the meaning of all this, anyhow?' he sputtered.

'Looks like it means, among other things, that we can just about write off Lane Branton as having to do with anything off-color,' Slade replied. 'If he'd had anything to do with what happened tonight, I sure can't see him delegating the chore to hired hands and not being there to supervise such an important matter, can you?'

'No, I can't,' grumbled Perkins.

'But I still believe somebody riding with the drive is mixed up in it,' Slade observed thoughtfully.

'But for the name of Pete, who?' Perkins demanded.

'A nice question, you find the answer,' Slade countered.

But despite his facetious remark, Slade knew that he *must* find the answer.

'I've been rather dubious about Branton from the beginning,' Slade continued. 'That's why I set you to watch him tonight; if something off-color happened, I wanted him to have an ironclad alibi.'

'Well, I guess he's got it,' Perkins admitted grudgingly. 'I can swear he's been in that rumhole all evening.'

'Exactly,' Slade nodded. 'So, as I said before, it looks like we'll have to write off Branton.'

'But how about that sidekick of his, Cliff Hardy?' Perkins protested, argumentative to the last. 'I've a notion that vingaroon would kill a man just for the fun of it.'

'He would,' Slade acceded. 'That is if the man was standing up to him. Otherwise, I'm very much of the opinion that anybody is safe from Cliff Hardy. I thought so in the beginning and I haven't noticed anything to cause me to change my mind. Hardy is a killer, all right, one of a peculiar breed, but I don't believe Hardy has ever been guilty of murder or ever will be. His kind have a code of ethics all their own, but a rigid code, and they live up to it. He would scorn to take undue advantage of an adversary. Very likely if he believed the other man had no chance against him, if he felt he could do so in safety, he'd turn his back and walk away. He's a real notch hunting gunman, of which the West has produced many, and there's no honor to be gained by filing a notch on your gun stock that you didn't earn by risking your life against a jigger who might well be as skillful as yourself. You saw an example of how Hardy works down there on the south bank of the Red. He believed he'd have a chance against me and was willing to take his own chances to prove it to his own satisfaction and that of ours.'

'And he made a mistake,' Perkins grunted.

'Yes, he made a mistake, but you have to give him credit for trying.'

'I still can't figure why you didn't drill the sidewinder dead center,' Perkins observed irrelevantly.

Slade let that pass.

'So I just can't see Hardy murdering John Lake and Pete Rasdale in cold blood,' Slade concluded. 'If he'd shot Lake and Rasdale, he'd have been boasting of how he downed two fast gun slingers.'

'Blast it, I'm afraid you're right again,' Perkins admitted. 'So where does that leave us?'

'It's leaves us where I think it will be a good idea to drop in the Lone Star and have a little talk with Lane Branton,' Slade said.

Perkins looked decidedly startled. Then he shrugged his shoulders and threw out his hands.

'Okay,' he surrendered. 'I've lived a good

life and I'm getting kind of along in years. Reckon it might as well be tonight as some other time.'

'I don't think it will be tonight, at least not from Lane Branton and his bunch,' Slade chuckled. 'Let's go.'

A hush fell over the big saloon as Slade and Perkins entered. In a swift, all-embracing glance, Slade noted that the majority of the Triangle B and T Bar W punchers were at the long bar. The others were scattered about at the gaming tables or on the dance floor. He spotted Lane Branton and Tom Ward sitting together at a corner table and staring in his direction. He sauntered across to the table, unconcernedly, Perkins following, not so unconcernedly and acutely conscious of the eyes of the Triangle B and T Bar W hands hard on him.

Branton glowered as Slade drew near. 'What the devil do you two want?' he demanded truculently.

'No sense in getting your bristles up, Branton,' Slade replied easily. 'We've had too much of that sort of foolishness already. I want to have a little talk with you, which will be to your advantage in the long run.'

'All right,' growled Branton. 'Sit down. Wait a minute till I order drinks.'

Slade and Perkins accepted the drinks. Over the rim of his glass, Slade regarded Branton for a moment. The rancher met his gaze unflinchingly.

'Branton,' Slade suddenly said, 'do you know of anybody to whom an advantage would accrue from having you killed?'

Branton's belligerent expression changed to one of bewilderment. 'Why, why no,' he answered, 'except my old mother, who would inherit the spread if something happened to me.'

'I think we can pass her by,' Slade smiled. 'Do you know of anybody who earnestly desires to have you killed?'

Branton involuntarily glanced at Perkins as he hesitated to reply.

'I think we can count Perkins out,' Slade said. 'There was a time when he would have been glad to kill you himself, but I don't believe he ever thought of passing the chore on to somebody else.'

'I guess that's right,' Branton admitted. 'I can't see Seth asking somebody else to do his fighting for him.'

Perkins flushed slightly, but did not appear displeased.

'But,' Slade said, 'somebody *is* very anxious to have you killed, or hanged for murder, either of which would satisfactorily erase you from the scene. And if something isn't done about it, and soon, they'll succeed, one way or another,' he added grimly.

Tom Ward's eyes opened. Branton looked uncomfortable and scratched his chin.

'Somebody, a bunch of somebodies, did try it down there by the Red the day of the storm,' he muttered.

'And somebody took great pains to arrange so that you could stand a good chance of being shot or hanged for the murder of John Lake,' Slade continued.

'Slade, what makes you say that?' Branton asked.

'Several things,' Slade told him. 'Among them the fact that John Lake and Rasdale were not killed where they were found, as everybody seemed to think, but somewhere else and their bodies placed where they would tend to cause suspicion to fall on you.'

'How do you know they weren't killed where we found them?' Tom Ward asked, speaking for the first time.

'The grass under where they lay was not beaten down by the rain,' Slade explained. 'Which meant they must have been killed before the rain started, or at least before it got going good. If they had been shot before the rain where they were found, the shooting would have been heard. Everybody assumed that the thunder drowned the sound of the shots, but it was already raining hard before the thunder got going good.'

'I'll be darned if that ain't right,' grunted Perkins. Tom Ward nodded agreement.

'In my opinion,' Slade said, 'Lake and Rasdale were killed some distance from the

137

camp. Doubtless killed by somebody they had gone to visit, perhaps in answer to a summons. Somebody whom they had no reason, so far as they knew, to fear.'

'How do you figure that?' asked Branton.

'The powder burns on their shirt fronts proved it,' Slade replied. 'Branton, you and John Lake were on far from friendly terms. Do you believe Lake would have allowed you to walk up close enough to practically shove a gun muzzle against his chest and pull the trigger?'

'I'm pretty certain he wouldn't have,' declared Branton.

'Neither you nor Hardy, or even Ward,' Slade said.

'But couldn't somebody have slipped up behind them?' asked Perkins, with whom to argue was second nature.

'Folks don't slip up behind other folks and then reach around and shoot them in the breast,' Slade answered contemptuously.

Branton and Ward grinned. Perkins also grinned, sheepishly.

'Slade,' he chuckled, 'have you ever been wrong about anything?'

'Maybe not,' Slade smiled, 'but if I start being wrong about a few things now, it's very likely that we'll all four have a chance to talk things over in the hereafter, and before long. I'm pretty well convinced that we're up on the board for speedy elimination. Branton, Ward

138

and myself for sure, Perkins doubtless because of the company he keeps.'

'Feller,' sputtered Branton, 'the way you talk has got me plain scared.'

'Stay scared, and stay alive longer,' Slade advised. 'Branton, did you ever make threats against John Lake, down in the Brazos country?'

'I never did,' Branton answered. 'I'm not in the habit of making threats against people behind their backs. If I have any threats to make, I'll make them to their faces.'

'That's right,' nodded Perkins. 'Lane was always that way.'

'I see,' Slade said thoughtfully.

'I thought for a while that John Lake brought you in to do his gun slinging for him, but of late I've begun to doubt it,' Branton remarked.

'He didn't,' Slade said shortly. 'I just happened along when I did; I was heading for someplace else. But now I'm here, I'm very, very anxious to find out who murdered Lake and Pete Rasdale.'

'I sure hope you do,' Branton declared fervently. 'It ain't pleasant to have folks all the time looking sideways at you like they have been at me ever since it happened.'

'I've a notion they'll stop looking before long,' Slade replied grimly.

'Any idea who did kill them?' Branton asked.

'I certainly don't *know who killed them,*' Slade answered evasively.

One of Tom Ward's hands called to him from the bar and he rose to his feet.

'Come along, Seth,' he invited. Perkins nodded and followed him to the bar. Slade turned to the Triangle B owner. 'Branton,' he said, 'I gather that your bunch and some other folks figure you and Clara Lake were planning to marry, before you had the trouble with old John. That right?'

'Rats!' scoffed Branton. 'I'd as soon think of marrying my own sister, if I had one. Clara and me were brought up together; we played together as kids and we've always been the best of friends, that's all.'

'But most folks thought otherwise?' Slade persisted.

'Oh, sure, they figured we'd get hitched sooner or later, because we were together so much,' Branton answered. 'But they were all wrong; we just never had that sort of feeling toward each other. Fact is,' he added with a grin, 'I don't think I'm the marrying sort. I've a notion I wouldn't pull over well in double harness. A girl from the dance floor now and then is about my limit, never anything serious.'

'We may have something in common,' Slade chuckled. 'And even if you hadn't had the trouble with Lake, you and Clara would have just remained good friends.'

'That's about the size of it,' Branton agreed.

Slade nodded and looked pleased; he was. All of a sudden certain puzzling angles were clearing up and he was beginning to have a murky notion of what might be back of the murder of John Lake and other things.

Cliff Hardy came strolling across the room and dropped into a chair. The ghost of a grin flickered his thin lips as he gazed at Slade.

'Where you been, Cliff?' Branton asked.

'Underneath a table ever since Slade came in,' Hardy drawled. 'I figured maybe he had something in mind and I didn't want no part of him.'

Slade and Branton both chuckled, fully appreciating the joke; Cliff Hardy was not the sort that would thrive in the atmosphere under tables.

'Looks like we're having a kind of get-together,' Hardy observed, glancing toward where Seth Perkins was in animated conversation with several of the Triangle B and T Bar W punchers.'

'We are,' Branton said, 'and I'm darn glad of it.'

'Me, too,' Hardy included himself cheerfully. 'I never did take any stock in these wishy-washy fusses; they just ain't my style. By the way, I heard tell that an outlaw jigger called Dutch Harry, who sets up to be some punkins with a hogleg, has a habit of showing up hereabouts ever now and then.'

'I understand he does appear in Dodge

141

occasionally,' Slade replied. 'Yes, he's mighty fast on the draw and a good shot.'

Hardy's usually expressionless face lighted up with a sort of malicious expectancy.

'Maybe he will show up,' he remarked hopefully. 'So long for a while; I'm going to amble around a bit.'

'He's going to look for Dutch Harry,' Branton observed. 'Another fast gun hand in the neighborhood acts on him like a red flag on a bull. He's a hard man but dependable in a pinch, and he sticks by his friends. Right now he'd gut-shoot any jigger who said a bad word about you. You're all he's been able to talk about since you shot that gun out of his hand down on the Red.'

'A strange character, but I've met a few like him,' Slade nodded. 'A throwback to the old berserker Norsemen who fought for the love of fighting. If Cliff Hardy had been born a thousand years earlier, he would have been perfect in chain mail and packing a battle-ax. Well, I think I'll emulate Hardy, to an extent, and do a little prowling around.'

'And I'm mighty, mighty glad you took a notion to prowl in here,' Branton said. 'I feel better than I have for a long time. Tell Clara hello for me if you see her. And,' he added a bit diffidently, 'if you run into your bunch, ask them for me to drop in and join Perkins in a drink with us; it'll seem like old times.'

'I'll do that,' Slade promised. He left the

saloon very well pleased with the night's work, so far.

Slade spent some hours wandering about the town. He stopped at the Dodge House bar, had a drink in the Alamo Saloon, another in the Long Branch, watched the dancers for a while in the Alhambra. In the Last Chance he found the Bradded L hands and relayed Lane Branton's invitation. After learning that Perkins was drinking with the Triangle B and T Bar W crowd and that Slade and Branton had been engaged in friendly discussion, the Bradded L punchers appeared pleased to accept the invitation and headed for the Lone Star.

After pausing at a few more places, Slade began working his way back to the south side of the tracks. He was diagonally across from the Lone Star when a man staggered out of a dark side street. It was Cliff Hardy, his shirt front dyed with blood.

'I found—Dutch—Harry!' he mumbled in a thick voice, and collapsed at Slade's feet.

CHAPTER FIFTEEN

Without an instant's delay, Slade went to work on Hardy, baring his wound, a bullet hole low down through the shoulder. It was bleeding profusely but there were no air bubbles to

143

indicate that the lung was punctured. Slade padded the wound with a couple of handkerchiefs to check the bleeding and bandaged it tightly with strips torn from Hardy's shirt.

The chore was finished and Hardy was muttering and mumbling with returning consciousness when three men stepped from the dark side street and stood staring. Slade straightened up.

'Well,' he asked, 'what do you want?'

One of the men peered with outthrust neck. 'We want that feller on the ground,' he said harshly.

'Why?' Slade askedd with deceptive mildness.

'Because he killed Dutch Harry, and Dutch Harry was our boss.'

'Fair fight?' Slade asked, his voice still mild.

'Reckon it was, but that don't make no difference; we want him.'

'What do you aim to do with him?'

'Hang him!'

'Well, you won't!'

The other stared, slightly nonplussed by the flat statement. His companions shuffled nervously.

'Listen, feller,' he said, 'We're three to your one and there's a dozen more coming up the street behind us. We're going to take that hellion, or else.'

'All right, or else,' Slade answered in the soft

and musical voice of El Halcon when he was most dangerous. His hands swept down and up as movement flickered. The air seemed to fairly explode with the roar of six shooters.

Seconds later, Walt Slade, one sleeve shot to ribbons, blood trickling down his arm, lowered his guns and peered through the smoke fog at the three sprawled figures on the ground. One swift glance and he began reloading with frantic speed. Down the dark side street sounded the pad of hurrying feet.

Slade glanced about. Almost alongside him was one of the big barrels of water placed at convenient intervals to use in case of fire. Dragging Hardy with him, he crouched behind its bulky shelter, peering around the swelling middle.

From the side street bulged a group of men, and there were nearly a dozen of them. Slade's voice rang out—

'Halt! You're covered!'

The bunch halted, with startled exclamations. Then a voice shouted—

'What the devil! It's only one man! Get him!'

A gun banged; a bullet chunked solidly into the water barrel. Slade's Colts streamed fire. A man reeled sideways. Another staggered, with a howl of pain. A third pawed at his blood spurting hand. For a moment the crowd gave back, yelling and cursing.

But Slade knew he was on a tight spot. The

odds were too great. One determined rush and he was done for. He cocked his guns and waited.

Across the street the doors of the Lone Star banged open. Out streamed two-score Texas cowhands. Somebody let out a yell.

'That's Slade behind that barrel!' he whooped. 'Let 'em have it, boys, let 'em have it!'

A volley of shots echoed the yell. Dutch Harry's outlaws whirled about and fled down the side street, two of them stumbling badly, others groaning and grunting from slighter wounds.

The Bradded L, Triangle B and T Bar W hands stormed across the street, taking potshots at the vanishing outlaws and surrounded Slade and Cliff Hardy, who was sitting up cursing.

Through the babble of questions knifed a stentorian bellow. 'What the devil's going on here?' bawled a florid-faced old man who came forcing his way through the crowd. He wore a big nickel badge on his shirt front; it was the town marshal.

'What's going on here, I say?' he demanded, shaking his fist in Slade's face. 'What's the matter with you?'

'What's the matter with *you*?' Slade retorted. 'Can't we celebrate Fourth of July a mite without you jumping on us with all four feet?'

'Fourth of July!' howled the outraged marshal. 'Fourth of July's been gone two months! Texas! I might have knowed it! You Texans ain't good for nothing except to cause trouble. Get out of town, the lot of you! Get across the bridge; and don't come back till you sober up! Get going, I say, or I'll fill the calaboose so full with you you'll have to spit up in the air! Get going!'

'Okay,' Slade replied cheerfully. 'Start moving, boys, the marshal doesn't want us here. He's the Law, and an honest citizen doesn't buck the Law. Two of you help Hardy to his horse.'

The grinning punchers filed past, two supporting the still swearing Hardy who nevertheless shambled along determinedly. Slade was about to bring up the rear when the marshal touched him on the arm. He turned to face the peace officer, on whose face was a quizzical expression.

'Son,' he said, 'I think I've heard considerable about a feller about your size and build. Yep, quite a lot. An old friend of yours stopped off here a little while ago and we got to sort of discussin' Texas and Texas folks. He got to talking about you, and once he got started, he couldn't talk about anything else. Called you "The Man from Texas". Described you so plumb well I could see a picture of you right in front of my eyes. Recognized you tonight, from his description, the minute I got

147

a good look at you.'

'Who was he?' Slade asked.

'A feller who cleaned up this hell-town a few years back, when it was ten times worse than it is now—Wyatt Berry Stapp Earp!'

*   *   *

After shaking hands with the marshal, who promised to look after the bodies of the dead outlaws and congratulated him for ridding the community of three such pests, Slade sauntered off chuckling. It was a small world, he thought. What happened in Tombstone, Arizona, cropping up unexpectedly in Dodge City, Kansas. Just went to show you never could tell which way the cat would jump.

The Texas cowhands clattered over the bridge, whooping and singing. Hardy hung onto his saddle horn for support, but manfully croaked his contribution to the uproar. Upon reaching camp, he was plied with hot coffee and put to bed.

'Slade saved your carcass for you by tieing you up and stopping the bleeding,' Perkins told him.

'Second time he's done it,' grunted Hardy. 'Hope I get a chance to even up the score.'

Slade did not ride across the bridge. Instead, he repaired to the Wright House and registered for a room.

'Hold on,' said the clerk as he glanced at the

name. 'One's been reserved for you, by Miss Lake. Front, show the gentleman to 301.'

Slade was being ushered into 301 by the bellhop when the door of 302 across the hall opened to reveal Clara Lake wearing something soft and clinging which defied masculine powers of description but the over-all effect of which Slade thought very charming.

'So you finally made it,' she said. 'It's nearly daylight. Come in,' she added as the bellhop shuffled off. 'What happened, anyhow? Your shirt sleeve is ruined and there's blood on your arm.'

Slade cast his hat aside and dropped into the chair she indicated. 'Just collected a few scratches,' he replied cheerfully.

Clara sat down opposite him, crossed her knees and cupped her chin in her palm. For a long moment she gazed at him steadfastly.

'She must have been a good deal of a woman, if that's a sample of her handiwork,' she observed.

'Think you could better it?' he grinned.

'Get me really started and you're liable to find out,' she answered pointedly. 'What did happen, Walt?'

'It's a good deal of a story,' he replied and proceeded to regale her with an account of the night's hectic happenings.

'It seems you are always saving my property,' she said slowly when he paused. 'I

149

suppose I'll be next.'

'I certainly hope not,' he declared fervently. 'Oh, the devil, I don't mean it the way it sounds. I just mean that I hope there will be no occasion to rescue you from danger.'

'You did once, at the Cimarron,' she reminded him.

'Okay, let's not have a repeat performance,' he begged.

'I came close to having heart failure that time when the tree swooped down on you. I'd prefer not to risk it a second time.'

'Granting that you have a heart to fail,' she commented. 'Of which I sometimes have my doubts. And you halted the trouble between the outfits and got them together.'

'At least I don't think we have to worry anymore about a range war,' he admitted.

'And you definitely believe Lane Branton had nothing to do with the murder of my father?'

'That's right.'

She hesitated a moment, her eyes inscrutable. 'And—and do you suspect who killed him?'

Slade repeated his remark to Lane Branton.

'I certainly don't *know* who killed him.'

'I see,' she said thoughtfully. 'But do you feel it was somebody connected with the drive?'

'I do,' he stated positively. 'Somebody connected with the drive either killed him or engineered the killing, which is the same thing in the eyes of the law.'

Clara nodded. 'I hate to think of somebody with whom I may have been closely associated being responsible for such a horrible deed,' she said.

'Naturally,' he agreed.

'Yes, a painful thing to have one's faith in somebody destroyed.'

'Life brings many a cross, who is without them?' he answered gently.

The blue eyes grew thoughtful. 'You are a strange man, in some ways,' she said. 'Yes, it may be a strange thing to say of one who appears to consistently live a life of violence, but I believe that in your heart you are deeply religious.'

'King David was a man of violence,' he reminded her. 'And so was Moses, and Joshua, and Gideon, and others of the great men of the Scriptures. The same goes for Saint Paul. Saint Peter sliced off a jigger's ear with his sword, and our Lord Himself used a whip of small cords to drive the money changers from the Temple. Sometimes violence is necessary if right is to prevail.'

'Yes,' she agreed. 'Not the least of the compelling forces in the world is righteous anger, and when, as in your case, it is exercised by one whose life is a continual warfare against the pests of wrong, it is well-nigh irresistible.'

'Thank you,' Slade said simply.

151

Again she regarded him, in silence.

'What you thinking about, honey?' he asked playfully.

'I was thinking,' she replied, her voice soft and sweetly slumberous, 'that it still lacks two hours till daylight.'

CHAPTER SIXTEEN

When Slade got back to the camp, he found the Bradded L hands in a hilarious mood. They were rehashing the happenings of the night before and bellowing with laughter when some humorous aspect of the shindig recurred to them. They gave him an uproarious greeting but complained bitterly because they missed taking part in his brush with the would-be robbers.

'Why the dickens didn't you tell us what was in the wind and keep us here with you?' one demanded reproachfully. 'Then we'd have bagged the whole nest of sidewinders.'

'Because I slipped,' Slade admitted. 'I figured they'd send two or three men to slide in and do a nice quiet chore of robbery and murder. I figured wrong—all, or nearly all the bunch must have come along.'

'Think it was the same bunch that tried to lift the herd down south of the Cimarron?' somebody asked.

'Very likely, I'd say,' Slade replied.

'Well, anyhow, we're thinning 'em out,' the speaker said cheerfully. 'Seven down there, four up here. Must have just about cleaned the whole bunch.'

'I'm not so sure,' Slade differed. 'Down to the south I'm sure not more than eight or nine made it back into the canyon, but last night there were almost twice that many. I'm afraid they've picked up new recruits in Dodge or someplace.'

'And you figure the one you chased that night by the canyon was the he-wolf of the pack?'

'That's my opinion,' Slade answered. 'Which means the head of the snake is still crawling around, and that sort of a head grows a new body mighty fast.'

There was a general nodding of agreement.

After sharing a cup of coffee and a sandwich with the hands, Slade rode to Lane Branton's camp to inquire about Cliff Hardy. He found the wounded man in good condition, propped up on blankets and smoking a cigarette. Hardy greeted him cordially, what he used for a smile on his thin lips. Slade shook his head.

'Why,' he asked, 'did you have to go looking for trouble with that blasted outlaw? And how did you happen to find him in such a hurry?'

'Slade,' Hardy replied, 'I wasn't really looking for him, and I was plumb surprised when I found out it was him. Happened this way:

'I'd been ambling around for quite a while, working sort of east along the river. I walked into a dive over there and the minute I stepped in the door I knew I had no business here. Pretty good crowd inside; a lot of 'em looked like honest cowhands, but I've been around a bit and I knew darn well they weren't. I didn't see any Texans, except maybe one. That feller was sitting over at a table talking with a big square-faced jigger. They were both looking in my direction when I walked in. The big feller just looked, but the other one, the one I knew, sort of jumped in his chair. Then they got their heads together fast and it looked like to me they were talking in whispers. I stopped at the bar and ordered a drink, but all the while I was watching that pair in the backbar mirror. Had a feeling something wasn't just right but let on like I hadn't noticed anything.'

'And what happened?' Slade asked as Hardy paused to drag hard on his cigarette.

'Just this,' the cowboy replied. 'The big feller got up from the table and ambled over in my direction. I watched him till he got purty close and then turned around. He stopped, and sort of looked me up and down. "Texas?" he said, "That's right," I said. "I don't like skunks from Texas," he said, and spat right in my face.

'Well, I knew what that meant and went for

154

my hardware. He went for his. Slade, he was fast, almighty fast, almost as fast as you, I'd say. He pulled first and he shot first, but he got me sort of high up and I slammed back against the bar but didn't go down. I shot twice and both slugs got him dead center. He went down. Fellers were jumpin' up all over the room, yellin' and cussin'. I went for the door fast as I could with lead slammin' all around me. As I hit the door I heard somebody yell, "Good God! he killed Dutch Harry."

'That made me go faster and I went up the street mighty, mighty sudden like. But I was bleeding bad and getting weak. By the time I hit the main stem, I was boggin' down. You know the rest.'

Slade nodded. 'Looked a good deal like a try at deliberate murder, didn't it?' he commented.

'Looked sort of that way to me,' Hardy agreed. 'I figure that Dutch Harry feller figured himself to be so good he could down me without any trouble. He was good, but like lots of jiggers who are lightnin' fast, he pulled just a mite off center, and after that, being better'n me didn't do him any good.'

'Evidently,' Slade concurred dryly. 'But why do you figure he deliberately set out to kill you?'

'I can't say for sure,' Hardy answered slowly, 'but maybe it was because the feller I knew wasn't just exactly pleased to have me see him

155

chummin' with Dutch Harry.'

'And perhaps anxious to make sure you wouldn't pass the word around.'

'Wouldn't be surprised if that was it,' Hardy nodded.

'Who was the fellow you knew?' Slade asked.

Hardy glanced about, making sure nobody was within earshot; he lowered his voice.

'Slade,' he said, 'I haven't told anybody yet, because I didn't know just what I'd run into and didn't want to be maybe doing somebody some harm. The feller with Dutch Harry was Curt Lipps.'

'Curt Lipps,' Slade repeated. 'Seems to me I've heard that name before.'

'Reckon you have,' said Hardy. 'Curt Lipps is Pace Goodwin's range boss.'

*   *   *

Again Slade repeated the cowhand's words,

'Pace Goodwin's range boss!'

'That's right,' nodded Hardy. 'I reckon you didn't run into him much down on the Red. Goodwin told me a steer jabbed its horn through his arm during the stampede the night of the storm and he was laid up in the wagon for several days.'

'And do you think he recognized you when you entered the saloon?'

'Don't see how he could have kept from it,

156

though he didn't act like he did,' Hardy replied. 'The devil knows he'd seen me often enough.'

Slade nodded. For a moment he looked straight at Hardy without seeing him; he was endeavoring to evaluate what he had learned, his mind concentrating on the matter to the exclusion of all else.

Of course, he told himself, the explanation of what had happened could be quite obvious. Perhaps Lipps had mentioned to Dutch Harry Hardy's reputation as a gunman of extraordinary speed and accuracy. Harry, a notorious desperado with a reputation for having a gunhand seldom equalled, might have, as his kind often did, decided to try results with another expert. Seemed ridiculous, but Slade knew well such an itch was not at all unusual amid the outlaw gun slinging clan. That *could* be the explanation of his seemingly senseless conduct.

But why the devil was Pace Goodwin's range boss associating with such a character, an outlaw leader with a price on his head in three states? But again an innocent explanation offered. It is easy to strike up a conversation with a stranger at a bar. Lipps might have just got to talking with Harry without the least notion as to who he was. Yes, that also *could* be an explanation.

But Walt Slade had a disquieting feeling that the obvious explanations were too darn obvious. If so, they opened up startling possibilities.

'How stupid can you be?' Slade muttered to himself in weary exasperation. 'You fix your eyes on the mountain top because it is in plain view and keeps intruding itself on your vision, and never notice the stone at your feet. That is, till somebody points it out to you or you fall over it and bust your neck!'

Abruptly he stood up; he wanted to get out in the open by himself, where he could think undisturbed.

'Hardy,' he said, 'I believe you said you'd like an opportunity to sort of even up the score where you and I are concerned. Okay, I'm going to ask a favor.'

'Go to it,' said Hardy. 'Anything you want done, even to pulling up green corn, spitting close to the house or pushing little chickens in the creek.'

'Nothing so bad as that,' Slade smiled. 'I just want to ask you to keep what you've told me under your hat. Don't talk about any part of it to anybody unless I give the word.'

'Huh! that's easy,' Hardy said. 'I never was much on talking to anybody. You're the kind of jigger that sets a feller blabbin' till all of a sudden he realizes he's plumb spilled his guts, and wonders why. Don't worry, I'll keep a tight latigo on my jaw.'

'Thanks,' Slade said, 'I appreciate it. Be seeing you soon.'

Slade left the wounded cowhand with his thoughts in very much of a whirl. In fact, he hardly knew what to think. It seemed utterly preposterous to associate the boss of the great trail drive and a prosperous ranch owner with the vicious happenings of the past few weeks.

But was Pace Goodwin as prosperous as on the surface he appeared to be? Slade had gathered from various sources that Goodwin gambled heavily, and a heavy gambler can be rich one day and darn poor the next. Such might well be the case with Goodwin. Also, all too often a desperate gambler will resort to almost any method to recoup his losses and be in a position to satisfy the feverish craving that gambling, indulged in beyond reason, builds up in the mind of even the most stable person.

Yes, that might well be the case with Goodwin. Carefully, Slade went over all he knew about Goodwin, which wasn't as much as he wished. He recalled how that when the trouble broke on the bank of the Red, Goodwin made no move to stop it until he, Slade, got into the act. It was as if he was perfectly satisfied for Cliff Hardy to kill Perkins and he and Lane Branton be killed in turn by the outraged Bradded L hands. That very likely would have happened.

Why would Goodwin possibly want Lane Branton killed? A plausible reason at once presented. Goodwin wanted Clara Lake, of that Slade was convinced, and the general

159

consensus of opinion was that Clara was due to marry Lane Branton. Little doubt but that Goodwin believed so, as everybody in the section apparently believed. Goodwin wanted Branton out of the way, hoping to catch Clara on the rebound. And for that same reason Goodwin stood to profit by the death of John Lake who opposed Goodwin's suit. With both Lake and Branton erased from the picture, everything would be in Goodwin's favor. Very likely he would get the girl and incidentally the Bradded L. Working on the theory that Goodwin was the gentleman of color in the woodpile, explained also was the constant harrying of the Bradded L, while the other herds were passed by. With the Bradded L crippled financially by the loss of the great shipping herd, Goodwin could step in and offer assistance, which certainly would not tend to belittle him in Clara Lake's eyes. Added to her admitted interest in the man, the element of gratitude would be introduced.

There at least Slade had the motive, and it is axiomatic with the Rangers to look for the motive. 'Find the motive and it will very likely lead you to the culprit.'

All of which was very fine, but the disturbing factor was that it was all pure theory with nothing of established fact to bolster his deductions. He could easily be making as colossal a blunder as he had in concentrating on Lane Branton. He painstakingly went over all that Hardy had told him. The fact that Curt Lipps, Goodwin's range boss, had been laid up in the wagon for several days after the night of the storm was of interest. When the raiders swooped down on him with the stampeded herd in the canyon, Slade was pretty sure that he had winged one or more of them when he returned their fire. Instead of a puncture from a steer's horn, Lipps might have had a bullet hole through his arm. More conjecture, but interesting, just the same. He resolved to try and learn more about Curt Lipps.

The opportunity came soon after he rode back to the Bradded L camp. He contacted Seth Perkins walking along the river bank, smoking and watching the hurrying water. Slade unforked and sauntered along with him.

'Seth, didn't you say Pace Goodwin was something of a newcomer to the Brazos country?' he asked casually.

'Uh-huh, that's right,' Perkins replied. 'As I told you before, he bought the Scab Eight from the Widow Harness and turned a rundown spread into a going concern. Brought in lots of good coves. He kept the brand and kept all the old hands to work the spread, but brought in Curt Lipps for his range boss, and Lipps is a darn good one, I never saw a better.'

'Lipps from Arizona, too?' Slade asked, his voice still casual.

'Darned if I know,' Perkins admitted. 'Don't ever rec'lect either he or Goodwin saying

161

where he was from. I think he's a Texan, though.'

Slade nodded, and deftly changed the subject.

CHAPTER SEVENTEEN

Even while Slade was discussing Pace Goodwin and his range boss with Perkins, in the back room of the dingy saloon in which Cliff Hardy killed Dutch Harry, Pace Goodwin, Curt Lipps and half a dozen hard looking characters were discussing Slade, among other things.

'Curt, I think you made a mistake in sicing Dutch Harry on Hardy,' Goodwin was saying. 'The chances are he'd just dropped in for a drink, with nothing else in mind.'

'I don't believe it,' Lipps declared stubbornly. 'I'm plumb convinced Slade set him to spying on me and the rest of us. I figured it right off soon as he came in.'

'And what of it?' countered Goodwin. 'Even if he'd spotted you talking with Harry, what would it have meant? Chances are Hardy never heard of Dutch Harry and wouldn't have recognized him if he had.'

'Don't you be so sure of that,' retorted Lipps. 'Those gun slingers all know each other. I figured the best thing to do was stop him before he could get back to Slade, and Dutch set out to do it.'

'Very fine,' Goodwin replied sarcastically. 'Just one little catch to it—he stopped Dutch, and he got back to Slade, all right, and Slade stopped three of Dutch's boys and punctured a couple more. And the rest of Dutch's bunch are sore as the devil at us and pulled out.'

'To heck with 'em!' growled Lipps. 'Just means less to share with.'

'You've got something there,' Goodwin admitted,' but one thing is certain, it's time for us to pull out. One more big haul and the girl and we're gone. We'll circle around, make Mexico and be all set. Plenty of fat pickings south of the Rio Grande and we can sashay back into New Mexico or Arizona whenever we take a notion. I've got some nice chores lined up for us later. The spread down on the Brazos? The Cattleman's Bank owns that, only they don't know it yet; it's mortgaged for all I could get on it, against the chance that it would be best for us not to show up there again. Let my fool cowhands go back and take over the running of it, if they want to. Yes, we're already sitting pretty.'

The range boss offered some excellent advice.

'Pace,' he said, 'why not light out right away without pulling anything else? As you said, we're already settin' purty. We've got the money for all the widelooped beefs we ran onto the spread during the past year, and for the five hundred Bradded L cows we ran off the night of the storm. We're well heeled, and, as you said, there's fat pickings to be had later. There's plenty more girls, too, so why bother with a pertickler one. And don't forget El Halcon is bad medicine, and he's on our trail. You saw what he did to Cliff Hardy. I wouldn't have believed it possible; and he's got brains as well as a fast gun hand. I don't know what his game is, but if I never see him again I'll be better satisfied and feel easier.'

'I'm not much on running from anybody,' Goodwin replied.

'Boss,' suggested an evil-faced young puncher, 'why don't you go to the lawmen here and tell them he's El Halcon, the outlaw? They'd lock him up and we'd be shed of him.'

'Because for one thing they might have trouble finding something for which to lock him up,' Goodwin replied. 'Nobody has been able to do that yet, according to all reports. Also, I'm not exactly sure he's an outlaw.'

'What in blazes is he, then?'

'I'm not sure,' Goodwin admitted. 'He might be a Cattleman's Association Rider. And he could be a—Texas Ranger.'

'Good God!' exploded Lipps. The others stared at Goodwin.

'But—but,' protested the young puncher, 'a Ranger ain't got no authority outside of Texas.'

'No?' Goodwin replied dryly. 'Well, Texas

Rangers have gone half way across the country and brought jiggers back, without requisition papers, just on bluff and nerve. I recall an incident of a Ranger following an owlhoot all the way to Arizona and down into Mexico, where he did for him. I heard that talked about over in Tombstone, Arizona, and I heard that particular Ranger described, which is what makes me think Slade might be a Ranger. The description sort of fitted him.'

'Well,' growled the range boss, 'if that chain-lightning gun slinger is a Texas Ranger along with everything else he is, I'm in favor of hightailing right now. I ain't forgot he put a bullet through my arm in pitch dark during a thunderstorm, right after when anybody else would have been squashed flat under the hoofs of those cows.'

'Even a Ranger can be outsmarted,' was Goodwin's grim ultimatum. 'Besides, I'm not saying he's a Ranger; I just said he could be.'

Lipps was still pessimistic. 'I don't like the girl angle, Pace,' he worried. 'You can do a heap of things in this country and get away with them, but putting a hand on a nice woman is something that sets everybody against you. Don't forget, there's telegraph lines across Kansas. They'll wire ahead of us and have the whole section on the prod; they'll head us off before we can make the Colorado mountains.'

A crafty smile stretched the corners of

Goodwin's mouth. 'That's just what I want them to do,' he said. 'I know how to leave a cold trail. Let them wire ahead! Let them ride! Before they figure out what's happened, we'll be in the clear. Put this in your pipe and smoke it—*I've got friends at Doran's Crossing!*'

For an instant the range boss stared; then abruptly he got the drift of Goodwin's statement; he slapped his thigh and laughed aloud.

'Boss, you're smart!' he applauded. 'And talk about nerve!'

'One more big haul, the biggest we ever made, and away we go!' chuckled Goodwin.

*   *   *

Along toward sundown, the Bradded L hands headed for town and a last bust before heading back to Texas. Slade rode with them; he wanted a look at the river saloons on the possible chance of picking up some pertinent information. He took the precaution to assign three alert young punchers to keep an eye on the wagon.

'I don't think there's anything more to worry about, but we're not taking any chances,' he told them. 'Keep on your toes and if any strangers show up who don't look just right, shoot first and ask questions afterward.'

'We'll do that,' they promised in unison.

166

An hour or two after dark, Clara Lake had a visitor; Pace Goodwin called at the hotel.

'Just came to tell you I aim to head back south tomorrow morning as soon as it's light,' he explained. 'I want to get away from this blasted town before there's more trouble. The quicker the better; I won't feel easy until we are across the Red. You can be ready?'

'Yes, I'll be ready,' she promised, and, falling into the trap, 'I think I'd better sleep in the wagon tonight, don't you? So there'll be no chance of me holding you up.'

'Yes, I think that's a good notion,' Goodwin agreed,' I'll ride across the bridge with you.'

'Okay, I'll be with you in twenty minutes,' she promised, and she was. Goodwin delivered her to the wagon, which was guarded by the three young hands, said goodnight and saved his triumphant grin until he was clattering across the bridge.

*   *   *

For several hours Slade prowled around the waterfront and Hell's Half Acre. He saw several of Goodwin's cowboys, most of them sedate and elderly men who had worked for the Widow Harness, the former owner of The Scab Eight, before she became a widow. Nowhere, however, did he see Pace Goodwin or his saturnine range boss, Curt Lipps.

Which was not strange, seeing that Goodwin and Lipps were busy elsewhere.

CHAPTER EIGHTEEN

The Cattle Exchange Bank was housed in a solidly built structure north of but not far distant from the Hell's Half Acre section of Dodge, on a quiet side street with an alley running in back of the building. The vault was new and of massive construction, so that the bank officials were quite easy in their minds concerning the very large sums of money habitually entrusted to its care. As an additional safeguard, a watchman strolled about outside, keeping an eye on any loiterers who might approach the building after closing time.

Not that the bankers felt there was much danger of a Plains outlaw bunch battering their way into the stout vault. Even the crude method employed against express cars and outlying community strongboxes, exploding a charge of dynamite against the door, would be of little avail and would only bring the ceiling down on the heads of the would-be robbers. Only a skilled cracksman could hope to open that door, and skilled cracksmen were at a premium in the rangeland.

So the watchman, knowing he was there for appearances more than anything else, was seldom much on the alert. And as he paused to peer down the dark alley behind the building, a grip of steel fastened on him. A hand was clapped over his mouth and he was held silent and helpless while a rope trussed him securely and a gag was shoved into his mouth and bound in place. Half a dozen shadowy figures converged on the back door of the building. A little expert work with a jimmy and the door swung open. The watchman, unhurt and treated gently, was carried into the vault room and deposited on the floor in a corner farthest from the vault. The beam of a carefully shaded bullseye lantern played on the combination knob and Pace Goodwin knelt before the door and skillfully manipulated a breast drill, changing the bits often.

The tempered steel bit into the metal of the door as if it were cheese. Hot shavings fell to the floor and it was but a moment or two before the drill slid through the outer shell of the door. The drilling evoked only a tiny sound, like a rat gnawing on metal. In less than twenty minutes the knob was lifted out.

Meanwhile the robbers discussed their plans in low tones that were nevertheless clearly audible to the watchman lying bound and gagged in the corner.

Pace Goodwin laid the knob aside. 'All right, give me the stuff,' he said.

One of the men handed him a metal container carefully wrapped in felt, another a small funnel with a long spout. Goodwin unscrewed the container cap and began, slowly and cautiously, to pour its contents into the funnel, the spout of which he had inserted in the hole in the door. As he did so, his hands shook a little and a few drops of yellowish, viscid liquid splashed on the floor. The men grouped around him gasped.

'For Pete's sake, Pace, be more careful with that nitro!' breathed Curt Lipps. 'If that stuff cuts loose, they'll have to take up what's left of us with a blotter.'

'Don't worry,' Goodwin returned imperturbably. 'I know my business. I didn't spend all my life in the West, and I learned this trade under the best soupman in Chicago. All right now, the fuse and the cap. Put this tin can over by the outer door, and be careful of it; there's enough of the stuff still clinging to the sides to do damage.'

Deftly he inserted the capped fuse, arranging it with the greatest nicety.

'Now the sandbags,' he said. 'That's right, bank them against the door; be sure this hole is covered. Okay, back against the wall; I'm going to light her.'

The tiny flame of a match flared and was touched to the end of the short fuse; a rain of golden sparks shot out. Goodwin hurriedly retreated to the far side of the room to join his men, who looked anything but comfortable.

Carefully smothered by the sandbags, the sound made by the exploding nitroglycerin was little more than a heavy thud; but the terrific force of the explosive hurled the vault door open to hang crazily by one hinge. Waiting a moment for the fumes to dissipate, the robbers entered the vault. Locked drawers and inner doors yielded to Goodwin's expert manipulation of the jimmy and other tools. Sacks were stuffed with bills and gold.

'Have the half-stick of dynamite ready,' Goodwin said in little above a whisper, which did not carry to the straining ears of the watchman. 'All right, that cleans her, and it's some haul! Let's go.'

The robbers trooped out by way of the open back door. Across the alley from the bank, the half-stick of dynamite, with a very long fuse attached, was laid down carefully, a match touched to the end of the fuse. A moment later fast hoofs faded swiftly away into the darkness.

*　　　*　　　*

Slade and Seth Perkins, along with everybody else in Hell's Half Acre and most of Dodge City, heard the dynamite explosion. They stopped in their tracks to listen.

'What in blazes!' ejaculated Perkins. There was a torrent of alarmed exclamations, then a

171

voice yelled,

'That was over by the bank! Something's happening there. Come on, boys!'

The crowd streamed north, shouting and gesticulating. Slade and Perkins followed at a fast pace.

When they reached the bank, somebody had already discovered the open back door. Men were pushing into the building. Slade and Perkins also entered.

'They busted open the vault!' somebody howled. 'How the devil did they get away so fast?'

'Here's Cale Abrams, the watchman!' another voice whooped. 'He's dead! No, he ain't, he's just tied up! Cut him loose! Cut him loose!'

The watchman was quickly released, the gag plucked from his mouth. Between sulphurous curses he babbled forth his story. Before he had finished, the town marshal arrived, puffing and blowing, and took charge of the situation.

'No, didn't get a good look at any of them,' Abrams answered his question. 'They had handkerchiefs tied over their faces and their hats pulled down. They sure knew their business-drilled out the knob and blowed her with nitroglycerin. Didn't make hardly no noise at all. But they must have dropped a can of the stuff outside. I heard a goshawful bang after they left. Go see if it blowed the hellions to pieces.'

172

The marshal sent men hurrying outside to scour the alley. He turned back to the watchman.

'But I know where they headed for,' Abrams crowed. 'They must have thought I wasn't listening or couldn't hear. They're headed west and figure to make Bear River Canyon tomorrow.'

'Bear River Canyon!' ejaculated the marshal. 'That's in Colorado, just the other side of the state line. We'll get the devils! Blount, Wetherel, hustle to the telegraph office. Send wires to Cimarron and Larkin and Syracuse. Tell what happened. The folks over there will head them off. Come on, I'm getting a posse together and we'll hightail after the sidewinders. We'll get 'em!'

The men who had searched the alley returned, having found nothing but a hole in the ground. Their excited babble added to the general uproar.

Slade touched Perkins on the arm. 'Come on,' he said in low tones, 'let's get out of here.'

Outside, Slade led Perkins away from the vicinity of the bank. His black brows were drawn together till the concentration furrow was deep between them.

'Seth,' he said, 'there's something mighty queer about all this. Why did they allow the watchman to overhear them discussing their plans? It just doesn't make sense. And why was that dynamite set off ten minutes after they

173

pulled the job?'

'Why?' asked Perkins.

'In my opinion, to bring folks to the bank and let them hear what the watchman had to say,' Slade replied. 'They wanted them to hear it, and believe it, just as they did. I'm willing to bet a hatful of pesos that our marshal is following a cold trail.'

'What the devil do you mean by that?' asked the bewildered puncher.

'I mean that they're not heading for Bear River Canyon nor Colorado,' Slade replied, adding, 'and I've a notion I know where they are headed. Seth, I believe you said the boys are at Long Branch saloon?'

'That's right,' answered Perkins. 'With Lane Branton and Tom Ward and some of their hands.'

'Hightail there,' Slade directed. 'Round them up and send them back to the camp in a hurry. Something mighty, mighty queer about all this.'

'What's worrying you, Walt?' Perkins asked as he paused before heading for the Long Branch.

'I don't know,' Slade admitted frankly, 'but I'm nervous as a rabbit in a houndog's mouth. Rattle your hocks, while I go to see Clara.'

When Slade reached the hotel where Clara Lake was staying, he got a jolting surprise.

'Miss Lake checked out several hours ago,' the clerk told him. 'She left with a big good looking man I didn't know. She knew him, all right, though. Seems to me she called him Case, Pace, or something like that.'

'Did she say why she checked out so unexpectedly?' Slade asked quietly.

'Uh-huh, she said the drive outfits were heading for Texas at daybreak and she didn't want to hold them up and was going to sleep in her chuck wagon,' the clerk replied. 'A mighty nice girl.'

Slade agreed, but he didn't waste time commenting on it. He said goodbye to the clerk and hurried to where he had left Shadow. Minutes after he was crossing the toll bridge at a fast pace.

As he reached the far end of the bridge, Slade heard a clatter of hoofs behind. He slowed down and a moment later the Bradded L hands and Lane Branton and Tom Ward overtook him.

'What's the matter, Slade?' the latter asked, anxiously.

'I don't know, but I'm afraid it's something bad,' Slade replied. 'Come on and don't waste any time; we're heading for the Bradded L camp.'

When they reached the camp, it appeared to be silent and deserted, and there was no answer to their anxious shouts. The fire by the wagon was still smoldering. Slade threw handfuls of dry grass on it and it flared up brightly, making the scene bright as day.

'Good God!' a cowboy yelled. 'Here's Wes Curry and Bill Talmadge! They're dead! They've been shot!'

'Where's Hartsook?' Slade asked, naming the third puncher who had been left to guard the wagon. A weak voice echoed his words—

'Over here! Over here!'

Slade and the others hurried toward the sound and found Hartsook lying in the shadow beside the wagon.

'The whole top of his head's blowed off!' gasped Perkins.

Slade knelt beside the wounded cowboy and explored the wound with sensitive fingers.

'Just a furrow plowed in his scalp,' he announced in tones of relief. 'Slug hit him hard, though. How do you feel, Hartsook?'

'I'm all right, I ain't hurt much,' the cowboy mumbled. 'I never did quite lose my senses and saw what went on. It was Pace Goodwin, blast him to Hades! He rode up with Curt Lipps and some more fellers. We didn't think anything of it, of course. But soon as he unforked he started shooting. Downed Curry and Talmadge before they could make a move. Another of the hellions cut loose on me and knocked me over. Reckon they thought I was done for, too; I had sense enough to lie still and keep quiet. Fact is, I was plumb paralyzed and couldn't have moved if I'd wanted to. Miss Clara came out of the wagon to see what was going on. They grabbed her but didn't hurt her. Lipps brought her moros and they tied her in the saddle. I think they got the money out of the flour bin—Goodwin came out of the wagon dusting flour off his hands.'

Slade heard a beast-like growl behind him. He glanced back. Tom Ward had drawn a long knife from his boot top and was fingering the razor-sharp edge. Slade saw that his face had become as the face of a wolf. His lips were drawn up in a terrible grin, showing the white teeth within; his cheeks seemed to have fallen in and his eyes glared, while his chest heaved spasmodically.

Astounded exclamations had greeted Hartsook's story, but Slade did not appear surprised; he began to deftly dress and bandage the cowboy's wounded head.

'Walt, what the devil does it mean?' demanded the bewildered Perkins.

'It means that I've been beautifully outsmarted,' Slade replied bitterly without looking up from his task. 'I was convinced Goodwin would pull something but I never dreamed he'd do what he did. He robbed the bank, of course, and found the money in the flour bin—somebody must have done some loose talking—and took Clara; he always wanted her. Well, the hand isn't played out yet and maybe he outsmarted himself. Perhaps we can take the last trick. See that your guns and rigs are in good shape; we've got a long and hard ride ahead of us.'

'You think you know where the snake-blooded devil is headed for?' Branton exclaimed excitedly.

'Yes, I think I do,' Slade replied. 'I'm willing to bet money he's headed for Doran's Crossing. Once across the Cimarron, he'll turn west and work down through New Mexico to Mexico, where he and his hellions would be safe. We've got to catch up with them before they make Doran. We'd have our hands full rooting them out of that nest of sidewinders. I think we can do it. They'll travel fast, but perhaps not too fast, figuring as they no doubt will that everybody's following a cold trail into Colorado.

'That should hold you,' he told Hartsook. He stood up and called the cook.

'Limpy,' he said, 'get your wagon rolling pronto. Send the wranglers to notify Ward's and Branton's outfits to get going and trail after us. All right, everybody set? Let's go!'

CHAPTER NINETEEN

Slade did not head into the cattle trail south of Dodge, although he felt pretty certain Goodwin was following it.

'We'll cut straight south across the range, holding to the east,' he told his companions. 'I figure that way we can make the river before

178

he does. Then we can hole up and wait for him, which should give us an edge. If we try to take him from the rear, he'll hear us coming and be all set for us or will speed up and maybe make Doran before we can overhaul him. Then he'll have the edge. We should make the Cimarron before mid morning, if nothing goes wrong.'

Mile after mile fell behind the speeding troop. The stars paled from gold to silver, dwindled to needle points of flame and were gone. The east flushed scarlet and rose. Groves and thickets changed from clumps of deeper shadow, took form as twigs and thorn points caught the light. Pale mist ghosts writhed across the prairie to dissipate as the light grew ever stronger. The sun came up in glory, banished the shadows and it was day.

Still the posse rode with unabated speed. The horses were sweating now, some of them blowing slightly. Shadow alone showed no signs of fatigue. Slade knew he would respond with a burst of speed whenever called upon to do so, but he held the big black in check in deference to the lesser strength of his companions' mounts.

The sun climbed higher; two more hours and many miles fled past under the drumming hoofs, and far ahead was a wavering band of silver ash that sparkled with shimmering glints. It was the Cimarron.

A huddle of buildings came into view, tiny

as doll houses in the far distance—the shacks and false fronts of Doran's Crossing.

To the right, a long line of thicket marked the course of the old cattle trail. Slade veered Shadow toward the belt of chaparral.

'I believe we're ahead of them,' he told his companions. 'I don't see any horses tethered around Doran. Looks like we're getting a break. We'll hole up at the south end of the brush and be all set when they get here; I figure they're not far behind us. With a little luck we'll catch them settin'.'

But the luck didn't hold and things did not work out in that convenient fashion. The cowboys skirted the fringe of growth and wheeled to the edge of the trail; and at that instant, a band of hard riding horsemen burst from the shadows of the growth not fifty paces distant.

Recognition was instantaneous and mutual. With yells of alarm the outlaws went for their guns. The air rocked and shivered to the roar of the reports. Slade went cold all over at the thought of Clara Lake exposed to that hail of lead.

But there was no help for it; he could only pray that she would escape harm. He caught a glimpse, through the swirling smoke clouds, of Pace Goodwin in the rear of his companions, wheeling his big dun and jerking the girl's mount around by the bit iron. Just a glimpse, and then Goodwin and his captive vanished back the way they had come.

Gritting a curse, Slade sent Shadow charging straight for the already demoralized owlhoots. His companions, yelling and shooting, thundered at his heels.

The owlhoots scattered wildly, throwing down their guns, howling for mercy. Straight through their swirling ranks Shadow tore, Slade guiding, upholding him with voice and knees while he ejected the spent shclls from his guns. Hc started to reload, got three fresh cartridges into one of the cylinders and grabbed frantically for the reins as Shadow stumbled on the rough track. By a miracle of strength and dexterity he kept the big horse from falling. He slammed the half loadcd six into its holster and gave all his attention to riding.

They covered a mile, with no sign of thc quarry; the encroaching growth was thick, the turns many and sharp.

'But he can't show us his dust for long, feller,' Slade encouraged Shadow. 'Not with a led horse in tow, no matter how good that dun is.'

They swerved around a bend at racing speed. And with all his iron strength, El Halcon hauled back on the reins, jerking Shadow to a rearing, slithering halt.

Not twenty yards distant, running toward him on foot, gun in hand, was Pace Goodwin. Even in that hectic moment of wild confusion,

Slade had to admire the cold nerve of the devil.

Goodwin fired. Slade slewed sideways in the saddle—there was no time to dismount—and answered the shot. But Goodwin was a weaving, ducking shadow. He fired again, and Slade felt the hot burn of the slug grazing his arm. Again he answered the shot, without results. Goodwin was only a dozen yards distant, now, andd coming on, shooting as he came. Slade took careful aim, but as he pulled trigger, Goodwin hurled himself to the ground and the bullet passed over him. With a whoop of triumph he leaped to his feet. The hammer of Slade's six clicked on an empty shell! Goodwin halted, his Colt jutted forward.

Behind Slade sounded a maniacal yell of fury. Past him flashed Tom Ward, his face the face of a madman. Straight into the flame of Goodwin's blazing gun he rode. Slade saw him jerk, reel in the saddle, jerk again. His horse gave an almost human scream and fell, drilled by one of Goodwin's bullets. Ward hurled himself clear almost at Goodwin's side. He leaped to his feet and closed with the outlaw. They went down together, rolling over and over in a frightful struggle.

Goodwin fired again and Slade, running toward the hitting, slashing tangle, saw Ward's body jerk once more. Then he saw the gleam of a long knife raised high in the air. Down flashed the steel and Goodwin screamed, a

182

horrible, pain crazed scream as the blade struck home in his body. Again the glinting flash, and again an awful scream from Goodwin. A third slashing blow just as Slade reached the scene. Goodwin's last scream ended in a bubbling shriek and he went limp. Tom Ward raised the bloody knife again, his hand wavered and the blade fell to the ground as he collapsed across Goodwin's body.

Slade knelt beside him, but Ward, shot to pieces, blood gushing from his mouth and draining from his shattered lungs, managed by a superhuman effort to raise himself on his reddened hands. He stared down at the corpse of his foe, spoke two gurgling words through the blood in his throat—'Got him!'—and fell dead.

Slade hurried to where Clara sat her patiently waiting horse. Her ankles were lashed to the stirrup straps, her hands bound behind her back. He quickly cut the cords and lifted her from the saddle. She clung to him, whimpering and sobbing.

'Everything's all right,' he comforted, stroking her bright hair. 'You'll be okay soon as you get the cramp out of your legs.'

'Oh, it was horrible!' she moaned. 'And he killed poor Tom!'

'Yes, he killed Ward,' Slade said soberly, 'and if it hadn't been for Ward, he would have killed me.' Clara shuddered and snuggled closer.

Slade gazed down at Tom Ward's face, which in death was strangely peaceful, and handed back the supreme compliment the young ranch owner paid him on the banks of the Red:

'A man to ride the river with!'

Around the bend bulged Perkins, Lane Branton and several of the Bradded L hands. They jerked their lathered horses to a halt and volleyed questions which Slade answered briefly.

'We got three prisoners,' Branton said. 'They talked. Four more with their toes turned up, including that blasted Curt Lipps. You were right, Goodwin and Lipps killed John Lake and Pete Rasdale the night of the storm. Came up to them just as the hellions came up to the boys last night by the wagon, and shot them down in cold blood. Then they placed the bodies where it would make it look bad for me. Part of Goodwin's bunch tried to kill Hardy and me on the Lower Trail south of the Red, and would have if it hadn't been for you. His bunch followed the drive and made the try for the Bradded L cows. Reckon you know everything, anyhow.'

'Not quite everything, but enough,' Slade smiled. 'Well, when the rest of the boys catch up, we'll amble back and meet the wagons. Something to eat and some coffee wouldn't go bad about now.'

Perkins was rummaging in Goodwin's

saddle pouches. 'Here's the Bradded L herd money,' he shouted. 'All covered with flour but okay.'

'And we recovered the money stolen from the Dodge bank,' added Branton. 'A hefty passel of *dinero*, all right, and a lot more that Goodwin got for selling the cows his bunch widelooped and drove onto his spread down on the Brazos. And what he got for the five hundred head of Bradded L cows Lipps ran off the night of the storm. All in all, a darn good night's work. Slade, the way you figure things out, you'd ought to be a range detective or a sheriff or something, instead of—'

Branton flushed under Slade's smile and Clara's indignant glare, and finished lamely—

'A maverickin' cowhand with itchy feet.'

The afternoon was well on when they met the wagons rumbling south and at once made camp. That night there was another freshly mounded grave on the lonely prairie. The simple head board read:

TOM WARD
HE RODE THE RIVER

The Texas cowboys did not stop off at Doran but crossed the Cimarron a mile to the east of the shack town and rode on south.

'I think we've had enough excitement for one trip,' Slade had said. There were no dissenters.

185

As they drew near the Red River, Seth Perkins glowered at the three sullen prisoners who rode under close guard.

'I'm still in favor of hanging 'em,' he growled, 'but Slade said no, and arguing with him ain't healthy.'

'He said to turn them over to the sheriff of Dallam,' Branton reminded him. 'Lake and Rasdale were murdered in Dallam County, you know. It isn't much out of our way. And he said to give the bank money to the sheriff to hold till the Dodge City people send for it.'

'Wouldn't be surprised if there's a reward for the return of that money,' Perkins observed. 'If so, Slade sure ought to get it.'

'I thought of that and mentioned it to him,' Branton answered. 'He just smiled and said if there was anything like that to divide it among the boys for a bust. He's a funny feller in some ways, but he stands mighty, mighty tall.'

'You can double that and say it again,' Perkins nodded. 'Yep, when they make his kind they break the mold.'

'But wasn't it the darndest thing, Pace Goodwin being mixed up in such a business,' commented Perkins. 'He always seemed such a nice feller, and he always seemed to be trying to keep down trouble between us.'

'Yes,' replied Branton, 'but as Slade pointed out, all the while he was really doing all he could to keep the kettle boiling. Insisting there was no proof against me the morning the

186

bodies of Lake and Rasdale were found was the logical thing for him to do, Slade said. It built up a case for him and kept suspicion from pointing his way. And when the big row was ready to break down on the south bank of the Red, he never did a thing to stop it till after Slade got in the act and shot Cliff's gun out of his hand. And Slade said that when he and Goodwin were talking together, Pace made out a mighty strong case against me while not appearing to do so. Oh, he was smart as a treeful of owls!'

'But not quite smart enough to go up against El Halcon,' said Perkins.

They crossed the Red a little before noon and were again on Texas soil. After the midday meal, Slade tightened Shadow's cinches.

'I'm heading east,' he told Branton and the assembled Bradded L hands. 'Got a little chore over there that can't wait any longer. But I'll be riding down to the Brazos country before long.'

'I don't see why you don't ride with us right now,' lamented Seth Perkins. 'Instead of mavericking off this way and taking a chance of maybe getting into trouble.'

Branton nodded emphatic agreement; but Clara Lake, smiling through her tears, whispered her goodbye with a woman's intuition and perfect understanding—

'I'll be waiting—Ranger!'